THE TEMPORAL

Stories in Time & Rhyme

The Temporal
Stories in Time & Rhyme

Authors

Asher Roth

David W. Brooks

Bungalow Stokes

Editors

RG Johnson

Asher Roth

Production & Design

Asher Roth

RG Johnson

THE TEMPORAL

Library of Congress Cataloguing in Publication Data
Johnson, RG, The Temporal
Summary: An anthology of short stories and poetry

ISBN-13: 978-0692510193 / ISBN-10: 0692510192

Copyright Acknowledgements

CONTENTS

Learning to Swim

By Asher Roth

"Any questions?"

The elderly man looked around the conference table. No questions.

"Well then, I believe that wraps things up, gentlemen."

J. P. Buckingham rose from his seat, removed his wire-rimmed glasses, pulled a monogrammed handkerchief out of his breast pocket, shook it open with a practiced snap and used it to wipe each lens—his signal that he considered the meeting at an end, and a successful one at that. "I think I speak for the entire board when I say that we have complete confidence in GlobalReach Enterprises and their management team keeping close tabs on the bottom line and seeing this project through to completion."

At this, everyone else stood and traded congratulatory handshakes. No hand was shaken more than Jack Albright's, who also received several slaps on the back.

"Way to go, Jack," whispered Fred Zimmer, Senior Vice President of Lease Acquisitions with Jackson, Fitch and Lundow, the principal underwriter for the project. "I think you nailed this one. Loved the equity amortization chart you tossed up there. Not sure it was completely kosher, but hey—what's ten or twenty million, right?"

He slapped Jack's back again, gave him a wink and walked off to shake another hand.

Oh, it's kosher all right, Jack thought as he collected his paperwork from the table. He'd spent the better part of last week working with his staff, poring over project forecasts and cost estimates on the Bradlee Brothers contract to make certain it was as accurate as possible. With any undertaking of this scope there was bound to be a sizable fudge factor, but he ran the data as conservatively as he could and it still came up roses. Surprised him, too, but figures don't lie...

"Jack, way to go! Bang-up job! I knew you had it in you!"

He looked up from his papers to see Nick Hargrove, Senior Vice President of Marketing at GlobalReach. Nick gave him a slap on the back. "I'm sure you know that I wanted one of my crew to handle this, what with the stakes being so high—but I gotta tell ya, Jack, and I mean this sincerely... I don't think we could've done it any better. I think you've got a career ahead of you in my department if you ever get tired of Accounting."

"Thanks, Nick, but I think I'll stay where I am for now."

"Your call," Nick said, making a pistol shape with his fingers and clicking his tongue. "Let's meet up later to celebrate. I found a great barbecue joint just west of town where the beer's ice cold and the waitresses are red hot—and, get this—there's pole-dancing tonight!"

"Sounds great, but I'm flying back this evening."

"Ahh... gotta get home to the wife and kids." Nick gave him a knowing wink. "Okay then, we'll postpone the celebration until we're back in Chicago. Or at least *you* will—me, I'm off to chow down on some ribs, thighs and breasts, if you catch my drift!" He gave a wave and blended into the cluster of suits.

Jack turned back to the conference table, neatly placing the remaining papers into his presentation folder.

Marketing—yeah, right. I'd fit right in with that group of losers. Actually, Nick's okay for a senior VP—maybe a bit too slick for his own good, and he grates after a while, but the guy does know how to have fun...

Thinking about Nick's offer, Jack regretted having booked an early flight. Still, it would be nice to get back home and unwind over the weekend... he hadn't spent much time with the kids during the past several weeks. Helen had been very understanding.

Then again, why shouldn't she be? I'm the breadwinner—I'm the one who brings home the bacon. All she does is watch the kids and clean house. How hard can that be?

He caught himself.

Yeah, right. That's all she does—plus all the grocery and clothes shopping, paying bills, cooking meals, doing laundry, and every other chore around the house. And she handles every crisis that crops up during the day—illnesses, scraped knees, bloodied noses, pet messes, broken appliances—and that never-ending parade of high school band boosters and magazine hucksters converging on our cul-de-sac like ants at a picnic. And she's a great mom to Jason and Jessica. Not too lax and not too strict; just the right balance of supervision and encouragement.

He recalled the day a week ago when he had arrived home at dinnertime: the familiar aroma of home-cooked chicken cacciatore greeted him as he opened the door. He saw the kids dressed in little smocks standing in the middle of the kitchen floor, painting pictures on their two-sided easel. Helen was busily shuttling back and forth between the kids and the cooking while talking on her cell phone with the doctor's office to schedule an appointment for Jason, who had a bad cough. Serious multi-tasking.

He wondered, if he was the one at home instead, would he have set up the easel and helped the kids with their painting while cooking dinner?

Not a chance. She deserves a break even more than I do. We should get a sitter for the kids, drive into town and take in a show this weekend. That will be nice.

He glanced at his watch: 2:45. His flight was scheduled to leave at a quarter after five. With the added hassle of getting through airport security, there was just enough time to grab a burger, get his things together and check out of the hotel.

Oh—and get something for the kids! Scratch the burger.

He remembered passing by a toy store on the short walk from his hotel, and calculated that there would be just enough time to shop on the way back to pack.

And for Helen? Something at O'Hare before I drive home—a half-dozen roses will do the trick.

*   *   *

Jack glanced at his watch for the third time, then back up at the board. The departure time for Flight 293 to Chicago had changed again, to 7:10pm.

Another hour delay—typical.

He contemplated getting something to eat. Even if the plane did leave a little after seven, with the connection in Denver he wouldn't get back to Chicago before eleven at the earliest. Plus, the time zone difference meant it would actually be midnight. But concourse food didn't appeal to him.

With the extra hour delay, Jack searched for a way to pass the time. The airport didn't offer Wi-Fi—even if it had, his laptop's battery was almost out of power.

He walked down the concourse to the airport bookstore to find something interesting to read. As he reached the shop, he scanned the newspaper rack just inside the entrance. It was filled with local papers.

Cat stuck up in the tree stuff—worthless.

There was a single copy of USA Today, but on closer inspection it turned out to be yesterday's edition.

He walked over to the magazine wall and scanned the display:

Glamour—*no.* *Cosmo*—*no.* *Vogue*—*no.* **Woman's Day**—*no.* **Better Homes and Gardens**—*no.* **Shape**—*hmm, nice bod... but no.* **People**—*no.* **Seventeen**—*don't think so.* **Field & Stream**—*no.* **Hot Rod**—*no.* **Newsweek** *or* **Time**—*maybe?... no.*

Next to the magazine display was a rotating paperback stand. As he slowly turned the rack and glanced at the titles along the spines, one caught his eye. Nothing about the book was exceptional, yet something piqued his interest.

There were several copies of the book. Jack lifted one from the stand, checking out the front. The title was in standard bold white characters against a black background—no illustration to give a hint of the genre:

Learning to Swim
A Novel of Our Times

By James J. Anderson

He quickly flipped through the pages: normal novel-style

text, about three hundred pages.

He looked at the back cover with several blurbs from reviewers:

"A revealing look at ourselves."

"Not to be missed."

"Engaging and entertaining from cover to cover."

Yeah, right.

He paid for the paperback and walked back to the boarding gate, found a vacant row overlooking the tarmac and sat down. He placed his carry-on in the adjacent seat, stretched his legs out and opened the book.

Chapter One
At Water's Edge

There was nothing to do but wait. It seemed like these departure delays were becoming the norm. Jack sat down in the black vinyl seat, stretched out his legs and started to read the novel he had just bought at the airline bookstore.

He laughed to himself.
Cute. Interesting coincidence with the name and all.
He continued reading:

He laughed to himself and thought: Cute. Playing on coincidence. What were the chances—maybe one in thirty that his name was also Jack? Probably more like one in fifty, at least. Another one in fifty

that he was in an airport. He quickly did the math—that was over one in two thousand... pretty good guess by whoever wrote this.

Jack turned the book over to the cover, checking the author's name again.

Anderson—James J. Anderson. Never heard of him.

He turned back to the first page.

Jack wondered to himself: who was this Anderson guy? Maybe he was using a pseudonym... lots of authors seemed to do that. Maybe he was a she. You never know. He continued reading, absent-mindedly rubbing his chin, which he did whenever he was pondering a puzzle.

He suddenly noticed that he was rubbing his chin and reflexively jerked his hand away. He blinked in disbelief.

Suddenly he caught himself, blinking his eyes in disbelief. He read a bit further—this sentence, actually—then he sat up straight and looked around the lounge.

Jack looked around the lounge.

What's going on here? Is someone playing a trick on me?

He noticed a security camera angled down in his direction.

Candid Camera? Am I on television?

He picked up his coat and carry-on bag and moved across the lounge to another chair. Sitting down and taking another look around, he stretched out his legs once more and turned the page. There was only one sentence at the top—the rest of the page was blank, as was the facing page.

Moving to another seat won't help.

This is nuts. How is this even possible?
He turned the page.

Maybe it isn't possible. Maybe you're dreaming. Have you pinched yourself?

He pinched himself, hard.

Maybe you need to do it harder.

He pinched himself again, wincing in pain.

Maybe you're dreaming about pinching yourself to end the dream...

Great. I'm dreaming about sitting in an airport pinching myself?

Dreams can seem terribly real. We can assure you that this isn't a dream, but that hardly matters— you could be dreaming that as well. That's how madness starts—the wall between reality and fantasy starts to fade, reaching the point where you have no bearings anymore, no way to separate the two.

Jack pinched himself as hard as he could, enough to blurt out a stifled "Ouch!"
Several people sitting nearby looked up for a moment from

their newspapers and laptops, then glanced back down as he met their gaze.

> **You might as well resign yourself to this situation, at least for the time being. You're where you're supposed to be, in the airport waiting for your flight, which has been delayed. Nothing weird about that.**

"Well *this* is weird, talking to you!" In fact, he wasn't talking to anyone other than himself. But the book was communicating with him, somehow.

How can this be happening? It can't be happening... not as it seems, anyway. It has to be a hoax... something I haven't yet figured out—like a card trick, or a magician's sleight of hand...

> **Nope. Nothing up our sleeve, Jack. No smoke, no mirrors. It is what it is.**

"What the hell does that mean: 'it is what it is'? It certainly isn't reality!"

> **Wrong again. This is reality. Or at least it's *your* reality.**

"What the hell does *that* mean? In *my* reality, books don't communicate with people. It isn't possible... not in real life!"

Jack glanced around the waiting area again, looking for a clue, trying to figure out what was going on, what to do next. There were about three dozen people seated throughout the lounge... maybe if he showed the book to one of them—to find out if they saw what he saw.

He played that out in his mind:

> "Pardon me, I don't mean to bother you, but could you take a look at this book? I think it's talking to me."

Yeah, right. They'd cart me off in a straitjacket! Even if somebody agreed to look, what would they see?

> "Uh—okay, mister—it says: 'There was nothing to do but wait.'"
> "No, no—read further down the page... right there!"
> "Um... it says: 'What were the chances—maybe one in thirty that his name was also Jack?'"
> "That's me—I'm Jack! My name is Jack! I'm that Jack!"

Oh, God! That would definitely get me committed!

Then another thought struck him: perhaps everyone else was in on the act—that it was some intricate setup, like the movie with Jim Carrey he had seen, where Carrey was unknowingly the star of an elaborate reality television show.

Yeah, right. That makes absolutely zero sense. Pure paranoia.

Is it?

Or maybe they aren't part of this... not knowingly. What if, like me, they're being manipulated, too? What if things aren't the way they seem?

What if this is some sort of alternate reality? Maybe an artificial reality... like in those Matrix movies. Maybe I'm caught in some ultra-realistic digital world, and I'm like Keanu Reeves' character...

what was his name? Neo? And Laurence Fishburne is reaching out to me to make me aware of the whole elaborate façade... that I'm the Chosen One, fated to save mankind...

He looked back down at the book.

Oh, come on! Drop the savior crap. You're not destined to save anyone. You're not "Neo". You're Jack Albright and you live at 35628 Summerdale Drive and you're waiting for a flight to Chicago that's been delayed for a couple of hours.

You'll be here for a while, so why don't we pretend that this is the book you thought you were purchasing and proceed with the story:

Chapter One
At Water's Edge

It was a dark and stormy night...
Let's try that again:

The night was dark and stormy...
Third time's the charm:

Dark was the night, this being a common attribute of nighttime, but in addition it was also wet and windy, or in the parlance of prose, 'stormy'.

Dirk Brigand stood upon the deck, bedecked in white muslin pleated shirt opened to the waist, sheets of rain lashing his taut abs that glistened like a handmaiden's washboard, his sinewed forearms straining to turn the ship's wheel as he grasped its firm, thickly-rounded spokes.

Jack grimaced and turned the page.

Suddenly, a roar emanated from the bowels of the crevice, followed by a thousand jets of flaming lava spewing forth and rocketing into the crystalline azure sky, each fireball arcing and then plummeting onto the frozen expanse with a crackling hiss and mushrooming cloud of steam. Fissures formed in the ancient permafrost, spreading along the desolate surface like the extending legs of a mammoth spider lying prone on the wasteland, tracing thin, haphazard lines into the distant bleakness that

Maybe it gets better.
He skipped the remainder of the paragraph and continued reading.

Meanwhile, in far-off Brisbane, Sister Mary slowly rocked in the porch swing, her knitting needles dancing their well-rehearsed steps—knit one, purl two; knit one, purl two—until she had finished and, holding them up in front of her, she exclaimed: "Won't Mr. Muggles be so proud of his new mittens!"

He rolled his eyes.
One more try…

"So, you understand the nature of this quandary, Fitzhugh? If we were then to assume that the equivalent par value from the procedure caused that departure from what we had anticipated the conjectural parameters to be, then it would follow that any reinvestigation of probable causes would not only adversely affect, but may in fact run contrary to, all extant theoretical models. Agreed?"

Jack reread the paragraph twice, then looked up from the book.

"Okay. I apologize. I'm not Neo—I'm just some guy stuck in an airport with a magic book."

He looked back down.

That's better.

He turned the page.

Chapter Two
Getting your Feet Wet

There are several ways to approach this challenge, the best of which is to first test the water. Become acclimated to the new environment. Try to relax— the last thing you want to do is tense up. We learn best when our resistance to new circumstances is lessened. Lower your guard.

Jack muttered under his breath, "Yeah, I bet that's exactly what you'd like me to do."

Okay, smart-ass, stay tense. See where that gets you.

A hollow BOOM suddenly reverberated beneath him. Jack jumped out of his seat and spun around.

Everyone else was still seated, doing whatever they had been doing. Several people were looking at him, some pointing and whispering.

An airport security guard seemed to appear out of no-where and approached Jack, his hand lightly touching the Taser holster at his side.

"Is everything all right, sir?"

Jack glanced at him, then down at his chair.

"Uh, yeah, yeah. Everything's fine. I uh… thought I had lost my wallet, but then I remembered where I put it. Thanks."

The guard gave him another once-over.

"May I see your boarding pass, sir?"

Jack handed it to the guard, who looked it over and hand-ed it back.

"All right, sir. Have a safe trip."

As the guard walked away, Jack slowly sat back down, whispering, "What the hell was the point of that? So you can manipulate sounds, too—just great!"

He looked in the book.

Actually, no. We can't manipulate sounds.

"No? But there *was* a boom. It even shook the seat!"

What's your point?

"Nobody else jumped. So you're inside my head now?"

That's a rather crass way to phrase it. We're not in your head. To put it in terms you'll best understand, we're an integral part of your experiences.

"So you're in my head."

If that works for you—although it suggests that we're controlling you, which we aren't.

Jack lowered the book, staring out the large window at the tarmac. If "they" weren't controlling his mind, then how could they anticipate his every thought?

Of course... time travel! They must be able to move about in time, knowing I'd be here at the airport, that my laptop's battery was low and that I'd go to the newsstand for something to read. Then they simply went back in time to set the whole thing up. It's the only possible explanation!

He opened the book back up.

No. Time travel—at least the way you're imagining it—isn't possible. Granted, it makes some enjoyable "what-if" storytelling: like the Back to the Future and Terminator films, and several Star Trek episodes you've seen.

But this has nothing to do with time travel—that is to say, actual time travel. Time can't be manipulated like space. It's not a "fourth dimension"—in fact, it has nothing to do with dimensionality. That's not to say it isn't intrinsically tied to space and motion.

Einstein was, of course, correct in postulating that the progression of time is dependent on the relative position and movement of matter. But time can't be reversed, and nothing can travel to the past or otherwise manipulate the temporal continuum.

Time is just... time. Sorry to crush your epiphany.

"Yeah, thanks," Jack murmured, turning the page.

Hey—we said we're sorry.

"So how are you doing this?"

It's magic.

He shrugged. "Okay, fine with me. That's what I said before—that it was magic."

We're kidding. It's not magic.

"Who is this 'we'? Are you some sort of committee? Do you have more than one head?"

Does it bother you that we refer to ourselves that way?

"So now you're psychoanalyzing me? You sound like a goddamn shrink!"

We were just asking a question. We're analyzing you every which way, but you've already figured

that out. We refer to ourselves in the plural because we prefer to. If it bothers you, we can refer to
ourselves as "I" and "myself", although that isn't really correct, either.

"Either? Oh come on, it has to be one or the other! You're
either an individual or you're more than one—there isn't any
other option."

If you say so, Jack.

"Okay then, tell me. I'm trying to keep an open mind here.
If you're not some entity or multiplicity—is that even a
word?—then what are you?"

Don't worry about it, you wouldn't understand.

"Oh, right... let's be patronizing to the dumb human."

Who said we weren't human?

"Well, are you human?"

Don't worry about it, you wouldn't understand.

"Yeah, keep belittling me like that. Makes me feel great."

The fact is that you wouldn't understand and we'd
be wasting time trying to explain it to you. Speaking of time, we didn't finish our explanation. Although time travel is not possible, time can still be
manipulated—in particular, its perception.

Imagine that you're a professional jai alai player and you're in the middle of a volley. Your opponent has returned the pelota—the ball—and it caroms off the front wall at 180 miles per hour. You're standing at the front line about sixty feet away from the wall, which means that the ball will reach you in less than one quarter of a second. In that one quarter of a second, your brain must direct your eyes to focus on the angle of the bounce, the path of the ball and its velocity and transmit this visual data in electrical impulses to your mind, which in turn must calculate the time and position of the ball as it passes by you. Neurons in your brain must then fire electrical impulses that, in a highly complex neuro-muscular sequence that is far too involved to explain here, cause chemical reactions at tens of thousands of relay points, which transfer electrical stimuli into mechanical responses in clusters of millions of specific cells, so that your feet, legs, torso, arms and head all move in unison to position your cesta—that's the wicker basket you're using to catch the ball—to intercept this projectile along its flight path and then to twist about in one fluid motion and swing the ball back towards the wall.

In order to do all of this in less than one quarter of a second, your neurons must transmit impulses at about a thousand feet per second.

Pretty fast. Faster than most people can clearly perceive or comprehend.

Now, what if that rate was ramped up a bit—say by a factor of ten, to ten thousand feet per second? Someone moving at that speed would seem to be a blur to most folks.

What if it was increased a hundred-fold? A thousand-fold?

What if it was increased a million-fold? A billion feet per second is about one hundred and eighty thousand miles per hour—the speed of light—which is the speed of electrical charges. So, what if there was a way to eliminate the chemically dependent synaptic delays and streamline the reaction time and movement to a million times faster than the fastest human impulses? Then, what took months to do previously would take mere seconds. Movements like those of the jai alai players that seemed lightning fast would be reduced to a complete standstill by comparison.

"Aha—I get it! So what you're saying is that you've sped up movement to the point that our relative motion—and thought—seems almost motionless, and you can move about in our world impossibly fast!"

Actually no. That's not it at all. Our ability to communicate with you this way has nothing to do with accelerated motion or thought. We just figured you'd be tickled by the notion. Good stuff for science fiction—much better than that ludicrous 'time travel' crap.

**And before you lapse back into your "I must be
Neo" delusion—no, this isn't some sort of alternate
digital reality controlled by some humongous
computer while your 'real' self is wired into an
endless nest of embryonic human chattel. Life is
what it is—the only exception being this book,
which defies your logic and will cause you no
small amount of frustration and torment.**

"I can't stand this!" Jack hissed, slamming the book down
on the adjacent chair. "Why are you doing this to me? Is this
your idea of fun, toying with me?"

He picked the book back up, flipping the page.

**No. Just passing time with a little intellectual rep-
artee.**

"Passing time for what?"

For the flight departure board to update.

He glanced up just as the screen flickered and the white
letters for Flight 293 to Chicago turned red, with the added
word: CANCELLED.

"Oh, great!" Jack muttered, shutting the book, grabbing his
carry-on and walking over to the Occidental Airways reception desk. A short queue had quickly formed in response to the
new message and Jack was fourth in line.

When he got to the counter, a perky young blonde flight
agent greeted him.

"Welcome to Occidental Airways! How may I help you today?"

"I just noticed that Flight 293 was cancelled. Why was that?"

"All we were told was that it was due to some mechanical problem. I'll be glad to book you on the next flight, if that's all right. We'll reimburse your ticket cost, of course, and provide you with a complimentary voucher for a future flight. May I see your boarding pass?"

Jack placed the book on the counter to reach for his pass inside his jacket pocket. The blonde glanced down at the cover.

"Oh! You're reading 'Learning to Swim'—I read that!" she beamed. "How do you like it?"

Jack stopped reaching into his pocket, eyeing the girl.

She sure was cute.

"You've read this?" He asked her, pointing to the book.

"Oh, yes! Have you gotten to Chapter Three yet?" She did an excited little skip and gave Jack a coquettish wink. "It's soooo, well, you know!"

He had no idea.

"What happens in Chapter Three?"

"Oh, I can't tell you that," she winked again. "That would spoil it!"

"I don't mind. Please tell me!"

She shook her head. "No, no, no! You really need to read it for yourself!"

"Just a quick description?"

"Nope," she giggled. "See?" She passed her perfectly manicured nails over her glossy lips, pretending to zip them shut. "They're sealed up!"

"A hint… anything…"

"Hey, buddy!" A voice shouted from the line of passengers standing behind him. "We all need other flights... chat later, will ya?"

Jack reached back into his jacket pocket, handing the agent his boarding pass. She scanned it and checked her monitor, her cupid-bow lips forming the most adorable pout he had ever seen.

"Oh, I'm so sorry. No more flights tonight."

"Can you check the other airlines? I really need to get to Chicago."

"Well, I'm not supposed to do that, but..." she flashed Jack a bright white smile and gave him yet another wink, "since you're a fellow James Anderson fan, I'll check for you."

Biting her lower lip bunny-style, the agent spent several moments typing keys and scanning her screen, and then once again did her playful pout.

"I'm so sorry, but it looks like our flight at 7:20 tomorrow morning is the first one."

"Okay," Jack sighed, "go ahead and book me on that."

She printed out his boarding pass and handed it to him. Now he had an extra twelve-hour wait.

"How about hotels in this area? Can you check what's available?"

"Oh dear, no, I can't do that," she answered. "There's an information desk in the lower concourse near the taxi station—they can probably help, but you'll have to go back through security to get there, I'm afraid."

"Okay, thanks," Jack replied, picking up the book and his carry-on. "I'll be sure to read Chapter Three."

"Oh, okay!" the agent giggled, winking at him a fourth time. "Trust me, you'll love it!"

On his way back to the departure area, Jack called Helen to tell her about the flight cancellation. He considered mentioning the book to her, but decided that there wasn't any way to describe it over the phone without sounding completely crazy. He spoke with his six-year-old daughter, Jessica, told her he loved her, and then with four-year-old Jason.

"When are you coming home?"

"Sometime tomorrow, buddy, around lunchtime."

"What did you get me?"

"Hey—my coming home isn't enough? What makes you think I got you anything?"

"You always get me something. Is it big?"

"It's big enough."

"How big is it?"

"It's big enough. Love you all. See you tomorrow."

He debated whether to find a hotel or sit it out at the airport. The seats in the waiting area weren't that uncomfortable: slightly padded and there weren't any armrests in-between, so he could lie down across them to catch some sleep.

He sat down facing the tarmac again and opened the book, flipping to where he had left off.

> **Your call, Jack. There's nothing wrong with playing Airport Hobo for a night.**

"Nothing right with it, either."

Then he had another, more disturbing thought:

What if this whole delay thing is their doing? What if I'm destined to spend months in this airport, like that Tom Hanks character in The Terminal? Or what if I'm caught in some eternal stuck-in-

the-same-place loop, like Bill Murray in Groundhog Day—not a time warp, since that's apparently impossible—but still, some sort of manipulation that keeps me trapped here forever?

Relax. We said for a night.

They haven't lied to me yet. And anyway, what are my choices? I seem to be at their mercy.

Am I? The only thing that's happened is my flight got cancelled. That happens all the time to air travelers—like when I was stranded in Buffalo for two days during that snowstorm. Hardly out of the ordinary. In fact, nothing is out of the ordinary... except for this book, of course... and that loud boom I heard.

"Okay, explain that one to me again," he said, glancing back down. The rest of the page was blank. He turned to the next page.

Chapter Three
Diving In

Jack stretched out along the seats and caught some shut-eye before the 7:20am flight.

"I did?" he muttered to himself. He *was* feeling tired, even though it was only dinnertime. Maybe jet lag was catching up with him from yesterday. But now the damn book was dictating his choices for him. That was just plain wrong.

Nope—don't think so. I think I'll take a stroll around the concourse, visit some of the shops and maybe get some coffee.

He stuffed the book into his carry-on and headed back down the wide corridor.

He glanced over at the reception area as he passed by, hoping to catch a glimpse of the blonde booking agent. She wasn't there.

Good Lord, she was cute—the way she'd bitten her lower lip, and that alluring little pout of hers...

He walked up to the reservations desk. The fellow shuffling papers behind the counter was a middle-aged man with balding hair. He looked up as Jack approached.

"Welcome to Occidental Airways! May I help you, sir?"

"Um, yeah... there was a young lady working here a moment ago, blonde."

The agent smiled. "I'm sorry, sir, but that's not much to go on. Most of our agents fit that description. I'm kind of the exception here. Did you need to talk to her about something specifically, or perhaps I can be of assistance?"

"No, nothing specific," Jack replied. "It wasn't anything important. Thanks."

"All right, sir. Just let me know if I can help you with anything else."

Jack walked away from the counter, swearing at himself.

What was that all about? What was I going to say to her if she'd been there? — "Hello Miss, that little rabbit nibble you do with your lip makes my knees weak." Why am I acting like some teenager with raging hormones?

He looked down at the book nestled in his carry-on.

They must have something to do with this, whoever "they" are.

He started to reach for the book, then stopped.

Nope. That's exactly what they're hoping I'll do—consult the book, listen to whatever they tell me. Just leave it there. Maybe even trash it. Find the nearest can and toss it in. Good riddance.

Then again, she did ask me whether I'd read Chapter Three... is that why I want to find her? To ask her about her copy of the book? For all I know, there really is a book called "Learning to Swim" by some guy named James Anderson—after all, there were several copies on the bookstand in the store. So... maybe she was talking about that book and not the one I have, and maybe the third chapter in her copy of the book really was exceptional.

Jack continued down the concourse to the bookstore and proceeded directly to the paperback rack, picking up one of the other copies of "Learning to Swim". He opened it and flipped through the first several pages—unlike his copy, each page was filled with the kind of descriptive prose typical of a normal novel.

He then reached Chapter Three.

Chapter Three
Diving In

Jack stretched out along the seats and caught some shut-eye before the 7:20am flight.

"I did?" he muttered to himself. He *was* feeling tired, even though it was only dinnertime. Maybe jet lag was catching up with him from yesterday.

Crap.

He placed the book back on the rack.

So... what does this mean? That her copy is some regular novel? Or... does she have my version and she's already read about my experiences at the airport, so she knows what happens to me in Chapter Three?

Or does she have her own version—a copy tailored for her that mirrors her own life and... what? Reveals something in the third chapter that is "soooo, well, you know!"

He didn't know. It was obvious he'd have to read it to find out.

Jack walked out of the bookstore and continued up the concourse, absent-mindedly entering stores along the way. He eventually found an eatery with pre-packaged meals and opted for a small salad to satisfy his appetite. After eating, he visited the few remaining shops at the far end of the concourse and then stopped in the restroom, washing up as best he could. Slowly heading back down the long causeway to the waiting area, he felt as though he was shuffling down the hallway at the state penitentiary; his feet in leg irons, a dead man walking to his execution. He knew that he was avoiding the inevitable—the last thing on earth he wanted to do was read Chapter Three, but his curiosity was overwhelming.

Finally reaching the row of seats facing the tarmac, he sat down, placing his carry-on on the adjacent chair.

He reached for the book, then stopped.

No. No way. Not in a million years.

He looked at his watch: 8:33pm. He set the buzzer alarm for 5:00am, and then stretched out across the seats, using his bag as a pillow.

It took him half an hour to fall asleep, watching the planes slowly taxi back and forth along the tarmac, but he finally drifted into a shifting gossamer of visions of his business presentation, his visit to the toy store, the taxi ride to the airport, discovering the book...

"Mr. Albright, can you hear me?"

A whispered voice, close to his face.

Jack struggled to open his eyes. He lifted his head slightly off the carry-on—his neck stiff and aching—and tried to look around. His eyes began to focus on the woman's face.

It was the blonde. She was leaning toward him with her hands resting on her knees, her ample cleavage in clear view beyond the open collar of her blouse.

"What time is it?" he mumbled.

"It's nine-thirty. I feel awful about you having to sleep here. Cheryl and I are sharing a room right near the airport and we decided you can crash there, if you'd like to do that."

"Cheryl?" Jack asked, blinking away the remaining cobwebs.

"That's me," Cheryl said, smiling. She was also leaning over, next to the blonde. Cheryl had deep red wavy hair that cascaded in little ringlets along her cheeks, with a face and breasts that reminded Jack of a Miss November he unfolded back in college.

"We just finished our shifts and we're stopping for a bite, and then heading to the room, if you'd like to come," the blonde said.

His mind clearing, Jack realized that he was still hungry. Plus, sleeping on a cot or sofa would be a lot more comfortable than the stiff lounge seats. Most importantly, it gave him the opportunity to query the blonde about the book. "Yeah, okay," he said, sitting upright. "If you're sure you don't mind…"

"Great!" the blonde flashed him one of her bright white smiles. "Cheryl and I need to check out through the airline staff exit, but we'll pick you up at Entrance B on the Arrivals level, okay? I'm driving a bright red Camaro, so I'm sure you'll see us!"

"Okay," Jack nodded.

The blonde and Cheryl skipped off holding hands. Jack

watched them until they disappeared around a corner. He felt like pinching himself again, but decided to leave well enough alone.

He picked up his carry-on and headed down the concourse toward the security gates and exit. Five minutes later, he was standing outside the airport at Entrance B, searching for the red Camaro.

Five minutes later, he was still searching.

And five minutes after that.

"I knew it was too good to be true," he muttered under his breath. He looked down at the carry-on slung over his shoulder and the book half-poking out.

What the heck… might as well.

He lifted the book out of the bag, turning to the last page.

Epilogue

The coroner zipped the body bag shut. Time to contact the family in Chicago to make a positive ID.

— The End —

The sudden blare from the car horn made him jump. He looked up, shutting the book and placing it back in his bag. The grille of the red Camaro was almost touching his leg.

Cheryl leaned out of the front passenger window.

"*That* woke you up! Come on, get in!"

She opened the door as Jack ran over to the passenger side, sliding into the back seat.

"You don't mind if we stop to get something to eat, do you

Mr. Albright?" asked the blonde.

"Not at all. And please, it's Jack."

The blonde glanced back at him and winked. "Okay, Jack! Enjoy the ride!"

And with that, she peeled out along the Arrivals lane burning rubber. Jack was sure they'd be pulled over immediately, considering that there were 10 MPH warning signs posted every few yards, but no one pursued them.

The blonde drove like someone possessed, first screaming down the airport access lanes and then the highway at speeds Jack had dreamed about reaching but never dared.

Cheryl plugged a flash drive into the car's USB port, and the Camaro was filled with sensuous, thumping rock, the driving bass loud enough to shake the seats. It reminded Jack of the sudden boom he'd felt at the airport. She then pulled a joint out of her purse and lit it, sucking hard on the jay and turning around to offer it to Jack. He shook his head no and she smiled at him, handing it to the blonde, who took a long drag. While she drove, the two girls traded it back and forth. After a few minutes, Jack realized that he might as well have shared it with them—the car filled with such dense smoke that he felt its buzz anyway.

About fifteen minutes later, the Camaro screeched to a halt in front of a single-story cinderblock structure that looked like a converted warehouse. The animated neon sign outside featured a girl dressed in a cowboy hat and bikini, sliding up and down a large pole. A multicolored light above the animation flashed:

WORLD'S BEST BBQ ♦ RIBS ♦ THIGHS ♦ BREASTS

And suddenly Jack realized that Nick hadn't come up with his parting comment.

What time is it? He glanced at his watch: *A little after ten. With luck, Nick isn't still here. How in hell could I explain coming in with these two?*

As they walked toward the entrance, Jack felt more than heard the thump-thump of pulsing music emanating from the building. He noticed that the parking lot was filled with pickup trucks and Harleys.

No reason to jump to conclusions—maybe they're here for the food.

Yeah, right.

He noticed that the interior of the building seemed completely dark, then realized this was because the windows were all blacked. The throbbing beat of the music grew in intensity.

The smell of beer and stale tobacco hit Jack in the face as he followed the girls into the restaurant.

Restaurant! A bar, certainly. A nightclub, probably.

Except for the few plates with ribs and coleslaw he saw scattered around some of the small tables, this was no restaurant.

Through the haze, Jack could see three silver poles extending from raised platforms to the ceiling, each one grasped by a young dancer wearing only a cowboy hat, bikini bra, g-string and stiletto boots. Each girl wore a ring of bills folded in half lengthwise and tucked into the strap of her g-string, forming a sort of ruffle around her waist. A hairy fellow wearing a leather vest and denim jeans with tattoos covering his arms walked up to one of the dancers with a folded bill and tucked it into one of the few remaining empty slots—the girl, still dancing, released the pole and grasped the man's head, guiding his face down to her crotch as she gyrated for him.

Jack took a step forward behind the blonde and Cheryl.

A beefy hand pressed against his chest.

"Forty dollar cover," said the beefy man belonging to the hand.

"Huh?" asked Jack.

"You a club member? Lemme see your key."

"I don't have a key."

"Then forty bucks, buddy, or you're bye-bye, get it?" The beefy man pointed at the door.

Jack hesitated, then pulled out his wallet and gave the beefy man two twenties. "Forty bucks! The food better be damn good"

"Oh yeah," the beefy man laughed, stuffing the bills into his shirt pocket. "It's tres bonne cuisine."

The blonde turned to Jack, shouting above the music: "Hey, we'll see you in a bit! Enjoy the show!" Laughing, she grabbed Cheryl's hand and they ran off together into the bar.

Jack was left standing alone at the entrance, probably the only man wearing a suit in the entire place—certainly the only one wearing a carry-on bag with a shoulder strap. His clothes would reek of tobacco smoke when he got home—they already reeked of pot.

How will I explain this to Helen?

He thought about leaving and calling a cab, but he had no idea where he was. Nick had said the place was west of the city, but that wasn't much help. And standing outside a strip club waiting for a cab at night in the middle of nowhere didn't much appeal to him.

Now he wished that Nick *was* still there with his rental car. Nick always rented a car, even for overnight meetings. He argued that, as head of marketing, he needed the added mobility in order to "scope out" each client's location—to see what the environs were like and get a taste of the local flavor.

Like this place. Well, no use standing by the door like an idiot.

He waded into the murky sea of blue collars and bikers, trying to find an empty table. After navigating much of the floor, he realized that every one was occupied.

"Hey! Down it front! You're blockin' the view!" someone shouted at him. He looked around for an empty seat nearby, catching sight of one a couple of tables away. Two brawny guys wearing tank tops and puffing stogies occupied the other chairs.

"Hi, do you mind if I sit here?" Jack shouted over the music.

"Knock yourself out," the brawny fellow closest to him answered.

As soon as Jack was seated, a waitress came up to him.

"What'll you have?"

She was wearing pink hot pants with nude pantyhose and a pink t-shirt with **RIBS - THIGHS - BREASTS** printed on the front. The last word was positioned across her ample chest, her nipples projecting underneath the sheer material. Judging from her figure and her makeup, Jack assumed that she probably split shifts between waitressing and dancing.

"I guess I'll have a beer. What do you have on tap?"

She let out a laugh. "You're new here, aren't you? All we got are bottles, and the only bottles we got are Bud. Take it or leave it."

"I'll take it," Jack replied. "And I'd like some barbecue. What do you have…"

She was pointing at her chest. "Just what it says, mister.

Although you gotta pay extra for the last two!" She winked at the two brawny men, who snorted their agreement.

"Yeah, Trixie, and worth every penny too, babe!"

"I'll just have the ribs for now," Jack said.

"Right. Ribs and beer. Got it." She held out her hand. "Pay up front."

"How much is it?"

"Thirty-nine with tax."

"Thirty-nine dollars?! How can it possibly be that much?"

She rolled her eyes. "Five ninety-five for the beer, twenty-four fifty for the rib dinner, plus tax, plus gratuity. You want it or not?"

Jack took out his wallet again, pulling out his last two twenties and handing them to Trixie.

"I'll bring you your change," she said, winking at the other men, who winked back at her and laughed. As she turned and left, it seemed to Jack that she intentionally swung her taut little backside in front of his face and stuck it out. He caught a whiff of her perfume and was immediately aroused by its pungent, flowery aroma.

"She smells good, don't she?" asked one of the men. They both let out a laugh and clinked their Buds together.

Just eat and leave. Where did the girls go off to? Nice of them to abandon me like that—finding them in this place won't be easy.

The last page of the book was gnawing at him.

What the hell does it mean? It couldn't be referring to me, because that doesn't make any sense—if the "story" is simply about my own death, then what does the whole thing accomplish? Is it a tease? Maybe it's a "what-if" scenario, showing me one possible outcome of future events, like the Ghost of Christmas Yet to Come showed Scrooge in A Christmas Carol. Maybe it doesn't have anything to do with me—after all, Chicago is a big town...

The song ended and the girl on the pole closest to him skipped away, replaced by another, this one with deep red wavy hair that cascaded in little ringlets along her cheeks.

Oh God, I should have known.

Actually he did know, or he had assumed as much, as soon as they had left him standing at the door.

How long was a stint at the pole? Probably at least an hour... with breaks, possibly two or more.

He looked around for the blonde but couldn't see the other pole dancers from where he sat, and he didn't feel like standing up to look around.

"Barbie!" shouted the two men at his table as Cheryl grasped the pole and waved to them. Jack was about to correct them, and then caught himself.

What am I doing? I just met the woman—maybe her name really <u>is</u> Barbie. At any rate, she probably uses a stage name—I certainly would if I was moonlighting as an exotic dancer...

Just thinking about that made him chuckle.

Jack Albright—by day a corporate cog, by night "Brad": an oiled-up thong-wearing male dancer. Were there any exotic male dancer clubs in Chicago? Sure, there were plenty of gay bars with dancers, but any that catered to women?

He imagined a seedy nightclub with blacked-out windows like this one, filled with husky biker chicks smoking fat cigars, chowing down on ribs and swilling bottled beer, ogling him up on stage gyrating around a pole...

He shook his head.

Cheryl/Barbie's marijuana must be potent stuff. It's certainly given me the munchies. Where are those ribs?

He looked at his watch. Midnight! He shook it and looked

at it again.

How is that possible? I haven't been sitting here for almost two hours... have I? No wonder I'm hungry. And thirsty. Where's the beer?

He looked around the bar for Trixie, and as he was turned halfway around in his chair, someone sat on his lap. He turned back around and was face-to-face with Trixie, sans beer or barbecue. Her breath smelled like sweet peppermint.

"The Boss says you like lap dances."

"Boss? What boss?"

Trixie didn't answer, pulling off her t-shirt in one fluid motion and revealing her marvelous pair. As if on cue, Cheryl/Barbie glanced furtively around the nightclub from the stage and then unhooked her bra and cast it aside, to riotous hoots and hollers of approval.

Trixie rubbed her own breasts and teased her nipples, causing them to rise. She rested her hands on Jack's knees and leaned back, her pelvis gyrating to the beat of the music, her crotch rhythmically rubbing against his.

Jack looked around at the other patrons, some of whom were having their own laps danced upon by other girls. He looked up at Cheryl/Barbie on stage: she wrapped one of her legs around the metal pole and smiled down at him. Straining to reach his carry-on, he pulled out the book, frantically flipping to Chapter Three.

Before he could find the page, the nightclub erupted in pandemonium.

"Oh, shit, they're here!" one of the brawny men swore as he jumped up from his seat and, with the other brawny fellow, quickly headed for one of several doors marked by a glowing red EXIT sign.

Within moments the entire place was empty, save for Trixie, who continued gyrating on Jack's lap to the music, seemingly oblivious to the commotion.

Seconds later, two sheriff's deputies were standing next to Jack and his lap dance partner. Someone turned off the music and turned up the lights.

"Okay, party's over," announced one officer as the other deputy grabbed Trixie around her waist and lifted her off Jack's lap.

"Hey, I got rights!" Trixie yelled at them, snatching her t-shirt off the table and squirming back into it.

"Not in this county you don't," replied the first deputy. He turned to Jack. "Sir, please stand up and turn around."

Jack did as he was told, feeling the cold steel of the cuffs encircle his wrists, the ratchets clicking until they were snug.

The deputy who had lifted Trixie from Jack's lap picked up the carry-on bag. "This yours?" he asked.

Jack nodded. "Yes, and that book, too."

The deputy picked up the book, which had fallen on the floor. "Oh, you're reading 'Learning to Swim'. How do you like it?"

Jack looked at him. "Uh... it's different."

"Have you gotten to Chapter Four yet?"

Jack shook his head. "Not yet. Why?"

The deputy gave him a smile. "Oh, I can't tell you—that would spoil it!" He dropped the book into the carry-on, and the two patrolmen escorted the pair out of the nightclub to their cruiser, its strobing light bar flashing red and blue.

The deputy carrying the bag put his hand on Jack's head, guiding him into the back seat next to Trixie. He then placed the carry-on in Jack's lap. "You need to remain cuffed until you're booked at the station, sir, so I'm afraid you'll have to wait on the book."

"No problem," Jack muttered. He wasn't so sure he wanted to finish Chapter Three now, much less continue on to Chapter Four. He'd never been arrested before: he once had a close brush with the campus police at college when they caught him peeing on the Founder's statue during Hell Week, but they simply took his name and address, gave him a lecture and sent him back to his dorm, and that was the end of it.

This was much worse. Jack had no idea what the decency laws were in the county, or what the possible punishment might be. He wondered whether news of his arrest would make it back to Chicago and how it might affect his job. Even worse, he was worried about word getting back to Helen. What had he done, other than go into what he thought was a restaurant to get something to eat? Then he remembered being awakened by the blonde and Cheryl, and taking them up on their offer to crash at their place—how would he ever explain that to her?

"You know, I could tell you were gettin' excited by my dance, Sugar," Trixie winked at him. "It's a shame we didn't get to finish the song."

Jack's face became flushed. "First of all, Trixie, or whatever your name really is, I had no idea that you were planning to sit in my lap. If I had known you were planning to do that, I would have told you not to. Second, I have no idea who your 'boss' is, or why he would have told you that I enjoy lap dances, since I have never had a lap dance in my entire life. And third, I had apparently been sitting at that table for well over an hour and you never served me my beer and ribs!"

Trixie gave Jack a hurt little sulk that reminded him of the blonde's cute pout at the airport. "Well, Sugar, I'm sorry about your order... I guess I got busy with other stuff. And it isn't my fault that they told me you wanted the dance—I mean, how was I to know? And anyway, you *were* gettin' off on it—I know that for a fact!" She sat back in her seat with a satisfied smile. "I know you liked my dancing, and as an artist that's all I care about."

Whatever. I have more pressing problems than having to placate this whore.

Never having been arrested, he had no idea what came next.

Would they fingerprint me—did they still do that, with the ink-pad and all? Would I have to stand in some sort of lineup? For what? To identify me as the 'perp', when they were standing right there watching me get dry-humped?—

"Ma'am, could you please point to the man upon whom you were gyrating in that nightclub?"

Granted, Trixie had probably sat on a dozen laps. No one else in a suit though... except maybe Nick. Of course... Nick!

For all he knew, Nick had probably enjoyed a lap dance earlier that night. Maybe "the Boss" had confused him with Nick because of the suit, and directed Trixie to give him a repeat performance.

Nick and I do look somewhat alike: same build, same color hair...

"By the way," he turned to Trixie, "I'm curious—how much would that lap dance have cost me?"

"Not 'would have', Sugar—*did.* You owe me fifty bucks."

Jack let out a laugh. "Yeah, right. First, as I said before, I never asked you to do that and I wouldn't have wanted you to.

Second..."

"First, second, yadda yadda yadda. You sound like some sort of fucking accountant. Is that what you are, a fucking accountant?"

"Well, I'm a CPA, if that's what you're asking. But I also have an MBA and I do quite a bit more than accounting. I review competitive bids and estimate costs for all incurred..."

"Yeah, well, I'M A FUCKING ARTIST, SO JUST SHADDUP!"

"Hey, both of you, zip it back there!" shouted the deputy from the front passenger seat. "We're here, anyway."

And indeed they were.

The station was an adobe-style building at the end of the street in what appeared to be a small town—what town, Jack had no idea. He could see bars on some of the windows toward the back of the building, reminding him of the jails he had seen in old westerns.

The deputy who had been riding shotgun helped Trixie and Jack out of the cruiser, walking them into the station and up to the booking desk near the door.

"Hey, Mike, what do we have here?" asked the duty officer behind the desk.

"A 288. Caught them doing the cherry cha-cha at Artie's."

"Tsk-tsk," the duty officer said. "And such a nicely dressed fellow, too." He smirked at Jack. "Bet you didn't even get your beer, did you?"

The two officers laughed.

"Trixie isn't the most reliable," the arresting deputy nodded. "She doesn't work for tips—not for waitressing, anyway."

As the duty officer began filling out an arrest sheet, the deputy removed the handcuffs from Jack and Trixie. He placed

Jack's carry-on on the desk. "He was carrying this with him."

The duty officer peered into the bag. "Laptop… charger… gum… tissues… paperback…" He pulled the book out of the bag. "Oh… 'Learning to Swim'! Have you gotten to Chapter Four yet?"

"I already asked him," the deputy said. "Not yet."

"Well," the duty officer smiled. "I think we can let you keep the book in the holding cell, if you'd like to keep reading. Empty your pockets on the desk here."

Jack did as he was instructed. The duty officer picked up the wallet and removed Jack's driver's license, using it to complete the form. He then slid the paper across the desk to the deputy. "Okay, Mike, initial it and book them. Put Mr. Albright in Lock-up B."

The deputy gave the other officer a quizzical look. "Lock-up B? Aren't the Gunther brothers still in there?"

"Yeah, they're still here," the duty officer nodded. "Maybe they'd like to discuss Chapter Four with Mr. Albright." He winked at Jack. "After you've read it, of course."

The deputy escorted Jack and Trixie to the adjacent processing room, where they were each photographed against a height chart and then fingerprinted.

"I've never been fingerprinted before," Jack remarked as the deputy inked and rolled each of his fingers in the corresponding digit box.

"Doesn't surprise me. You don't strike me as the kind who gets arrested too often. Sorry about the ink—we're getting a scanner next month."

For some reason, Jack felt a sense of pride at being one of the last to be booked by the old method.

Something to tell my kids when they're old enough.

Or not.

After processing, Trixie was escorted by a female officer to another section of the station, and the deputy walked Jack through a small sally port into the holding cell area. There were two large cells with bars extending from ceiling to floor, and a series of smaller cell rooms along the wall. The first barred cell was vacant. Two huge, burly men wearing tank tops, jeans and combat boots, their bodies covered with tattoos, occupied the second large cell.

The deputy unlocked the second cell door and slid it open, handing Jack the book. "Enjoy your stay."

"Wait a minute… aren't I supposed to get a phone call? How am I going to contact my lawyer?"

"Do you have a lawyer?"

Jack didn't. Some of his friends were lawyers, but they weren't criminal defense attorneys—they specialized in things like patent law and bankruptcies. Then there were the corporate attorneys at work, but they wouldn't be of any help in this situation. He could call Helen and ask her to find an attorney for him, but that was out of the question—the last thing he wanted was for her to find out about this.

The deputy sighed impatiently. "Look… you'll be out of here soon enough. The judge'll set bail and after you post it you can walk."

"But I've got a seven-twenty flight in the morning. What time is it?"

The deputy pointed to a large wall clock. "One twenty-four. You should've thought about that before your midnight dance at Artie's." He pushed Jack into the cell and slammed the door shut with a resounding clang.

Jack glanced warily at the two massive men who were eyeing him from across the cell. He went to the far corner and sat down on the floor: the smooth concrete surface felt cool and reeked of urine, and he wondered what he was sitting in, but at this point he didn't care—all that mattered was reading the book.

He frantically flipped through the pages, bypassing the rest of Chapter Three.

Chapter Four
Different Strokes for Different Folks

Jack was not in a good mood.

"Thanks for telling me," he muttered to himself. He glanced up at the clock on the wall again, then back down.

He glanced up at the clock. 1:25am. Less than six hours to gain release from this jail in this God-forsaken town in the middle of nowhere and then make it back to the airport to catch his flight.

He sifted back through the events of the past few hours, trying to figure out how he had ended up in this predicament. The arrest at the strip joint... the pot-smoke-filled car ride... being awakened at the airport... thinking the blonde was cute... purchasing this book. More than anything, he wanted to blame this book. Somehow, it was controlling him, guiding him down this pathway like a rat in a maze.

He was convinced that it could manipulate his per-

ception: for example, that jarring boom he had heard when he was sitting in the airport. What hadn't occurred to Jack, because his perspective was so skewed by unmitigated paranoia, was that there actually *had* been a loud sound, caused by a malfunctioning luggage conveyor directly underneath the waiting area. The other passengers sitting near Jack were also startled by the noise—but their reactions had been more subdued and controlled, because the same sound had occurred several minutes earlier while Jack was in the bookstore purchasing this book. Having heard the prior bang, they surmised that it must be a recurring event. At any rate, they hadn't jumped out of their seats like some crazed psycho, catching the attention of the airport security guard.

You know, Jack, you're turning into a real disappointment. We expected you to be shocked by all of this—after all, it runs counter to your delicate grasp of reality. But we figured you to be smart enough to adapt to new circumstances.

"I can adapt—I'm good at dealing with new situations."

We'll see.

There was a time, not too long ago, when humans regarded everything as property. The land that they lived on and lived off was, of course, their property. So was everything on this land: the water, minerals, wildlife, crops, homes, furnishings, tools—even their wives were considered their property.

Wives, however, didn't consider their husbands to be *their* property. Possession, you see, is based on power. In the case of human property, it's based primarily on physical power.

"Looky what we got here," one of the Gunther brothers said.

Jack looked up. Both of the men were standing over him, eyeing him. The one who had spoken knelt down and played with Jack's hair with his immense hand. "He sure is a purty thang."

"I bet he got nice silky hair all over his body," his brother remarked.

"Yeah, all nice an' soft an' silky!" the squatting man agreed.

The standing Gunther squatted next to his brother. Jack could see that half of his teeth were missing and the others were rotted yellow. His breath was worse than the urine-soaked floor.

"Listen, boy, we like you a lot, an' we aim t' find out if you does have silky hair all over your sweet li'l self, but first we like t' get acquainted with our cellmates, if'n you know what I mean."

He looked over at his brother and winked, then turned back to Jack. "You ever service a man before, boy?"

Service a man—what a polite way to put it.

Jack had never serviced a man. The very thought was so repulsive to him that he felt he'd rather die than service a man.

Both men stood back up and unzipped their flies.

"Now, boy, we'll start off real easy-like. Me an' my brother wants you to reach in here an' make us happy, both at the same time. We wanna see who you can make happiest first."

Jack didn't move.

One of the brothers grasped Jack by the hair and violently yanked it backward, so that Jack was looking up at him.

"What, you deaf, boy? My brother jus' told you what we want you to do. You wanna be our friend, don't you, boy? You don't wanna make us angry, unnerstan'?" He released the clump of hair, snapping Jack's head back forward. "Let's go, boy!"

Jack's mind was racing. There was no way in hell that he would do what they wanted, but he didn't see any way out of getting pummeled when he refused.

Pummeled... right. More like beaten to within an inch of my life and then raped repeatedly. These Neanderthals aren't just looking to get their rocks off—they want to pleasure themselves crushing me, turning me into bloody goop to be scraped off the floor with the urine and scum.

A plan—I need a plan. A plan of attack... hurt them as much as I can before they butcher me. Reach up and grab both of their dicks like they want me to—then yank like no tomorrow—enough pain to throw them off balance, then punch fast—aim for their Adam's apples—try to crush their windpipes and then scream like a goddamn howler monkey in heat for the deputy.

As Jack started to reach up, his eye caught the book lying open on the cell floor.

Screw your plan — *SCREAM NOW!*

Jack screamed. He screamed louder than he had ever screamed in his life. He screamed like he had been stabbed in the gut, like someone was drilling a hole into his skull, like it was *his* dick being torn off his body.

The two brothers covered their ears, wincing in pain. Jack couldn't hear them over his scream, but they seemed to be yelling "SHIT!"

The deputy ran into the holding cell area brandishing a shotgun. "What the fuck!" he yelled at Jack, who stopped screaming. "You sounded like... like..."

"... like someone going to be raped?" Jack tried to finish the deputy's thought, but his throat hurt too much. After a moment he managed to croak: "Get me the hell out of this cell and let me call my lawyer NOW."

The deputy opened the cell door as Jack scooped up the book. He escorted Jack back out through the sally port to a small office with a phone. Jack still had no idea who to call— finally deciding on Arnie Rombauer, an old college buddy, simply because he knew that Arnie had used an attorney for his divorce, and he happened to know Arnie's home number.

The phone rang several times before a very tired voice answered: "Hell... hello? Who is this?"

"Hey, Arnie." Jack croaked.

"Who is this? What time is it?"

Jack looked up at the office wall clock: 1:45am... which meant that it was a quarter to four back in Chicago. Stricken by guilt for waking his friend, he hung up the phone, then immediately regretted hanging up. He started dialing the number again.

The deputy grabbed the handpiece from Jack and placed it back on its cradle. "You only get one call."

"But I didn't speak to anyone!"

"Yes, you did."

"No, I didn't. Not really."

"Did your call go through?"

"Yes, but…"

"One call. Come on, let's go."

Protesting along the way, Jack was led back into the holding cell area. Instead of walking Jack back to Lock-up B, the deputy opened one of the small walled cells.

"In you go. You can scream in here all night if you want."

He slammed the door shut behind Jack.

Alone in the cell away from the Gunther brothers, Jack felt completely relieved. He realized that he'd been holding himself ever since the bust at the pole-dancing joint. After urinating in the cell's steel toilet, he sat down on the hard bunk bed, opened the book and started reading again.

At least you're not playing pump the pepperoni with Ike and Mike anymore.

They knew that was going to happen. They knew about everything that's happened to me tonight! What sort of game is this?

It's not a game. Unless, of course, you consider life to be a game—which isn't such a bad approach: life certainly has its share of challenges. The problem with that perspective, though, is that it frames life as a competition, leading to either victory or defeat. Even if you regard it as some sort of friendly game, like pat-a-cake or Double Dutch jump rope, it still has you preoccupied with reaching a goal,

rather than embracing the experience.

It's best to think of life as a journey... not to any particular destination—just a walk in the woods, so to speak. Along the way, you encounter new things, have new experiences and, with luck, you even learn a thing or two about the world, and about yourself.

"What's the sense of that if I'm going to die anyway? Tell me about the epilogue!"

Ever since Jack had turned to the last page of this book and read the short epilogue, he'd been pondering its meaning. Was he the person in the body bag? If so, what was the purpose of this book—of this whole absurd "journey"—of anything, for that matter?

Psychologists have a name for people who insist on reading the end of novels at the start. They are known as BPDs or Borderline Personality Disorders. They are impatient, impulsive, and anxious to arrive at the end of every situation, without wasting time getting there. They consider the story itself to be immaterial. All that matters to them is the conclusion.

Then again, maybe they're just curious... especially if the novel is about them. It's certainly understandable that, if someone had in their possession a book detailing their life, they'd want to flip ahead and find out what happens. Never mind that they can't change it—once it's in print, that's tanta-mount to being engraved in stone. If it says that something terrible happens and they're paralyzed, or they have cancer, or they lose an eye or a limb or even their life, is it better to know this ahead of time?

Ignorance can be blissful. The journey is much more enjoyable and fulfilling—perhaps even more enlightening—when you don't know what lies ahead. The destination is unimportant... it's best to sit back and enjoy the ride.

"But in real life I *have* a destination—Chicago... my fami-ly... my job.... and you seem intent on preventing me from getting there!"

Excuse us—how have we prevented you from get-ting anywhere?

"You had nothing to do with canceling the flight, is that what you're telling me?"

Airline flights get cancelled all the time.

"And you didn't have that blonde stripper wake me up and invite me to her place?"

She wasn't a plant, if that's what you're asking. She's just a very cute airline reservations clerk who moonlights as an exotic dancer in a local night-club, who took pity on you and offered you a place to stay for the night.

"Which we never reached. So you had nothing to do with the police bust, either?"

Look, we realize that this night probably hasn't been your average night. But we're not creating these circumstances—you've done a perfectly good job of that yourself.

Think of it as pathways along a very intricate network of possibilities: the neural network analogy we discussed earlier works fine here. Imagine that you, Jack Albright, are a neural impulse traveling along a nerve cell, and you come to a synapse. This synapse connects to several other nerve cells, and as you leap across the synaptic void you select which nerve to follow. You travel a short distance, approach another synapse and you jump and select again, and so on. You're traveling down a specific pathway of your choosing among a virtually infinite number of possibilities.

You could have stood up, dumping Trixie, and run for the exits like everyone else. You could have pushed Trixie off your lap before she started her dance. You could have kept better track of the time and left the nightclub instead of waiting two hours for your ribs and beer. You could have left the club when you first arrived and hailed a cab and made it back to the airport. You could have politely turned down the reservations agents' offer to sleep at their apartment. You could have found a hotel instead of deciding to sleep at the departure gate.

"Wait right there—you told me that was a wise choice!"

Correction: we told you that there was nothing wrong with your choice. Big difference. The point is that you made these choices, Jack, not us. And these were just the major choices—there are thousands of smaller choices along the way: whether to skip the ribs and just order a beer, or not order anything at all; which table to sit at, or not sit down at all; how deeply to inhale the pot smoke in the car; whether to pick your nose right now...

Jack realized that his finger was about to enter his nostril and quickly pulled it away.

Everything you do, no matter how small and inconsequential it may seem, has repercussions. It sends you down a pathway that leads in a direction different from any alternate route you may have chosen.

"But why me? Why is my life so important?"

Excuse us?

"Why me?"

Why you what?

"Well, it's obvious that you wanted me to read this book.

None of this conversation we're having... it isn't really a conversation—I'm not even sure what it is we're having—but none of it would be happening if I hadn't picked up the book, right?"

And your point is...?

"Well, you must have singled me out for some reason."

Did we tell you to buy this book?

"No, of course not."

Are you the only one who has read this book?

"No... the blonde said that she read it. And the deputy. And the officer at the desk."

So you haven't been singled out.

"But I don't know what they read. It can't be the same thing I'm reading."

Maybe, maybe not. You already did some thinking on this when you went back to the bookstore. The toss-up was that you have no idea what they read or whether it relates in any way to what you're reading. In truth, it doesn't matter what they read. It's completely immaterial.

"So I *have* been singled out."

Maybe *they* were the ones who were singled out.

"*They* were singled out and not *me*? Is that what you're saying?" Jack thought about this, trying to twist his mind around it:

The others were singled out, and yet what they read apparently has no bearing on what I'm reading, since I wasn't singled out. Even so, their mentioning to me that they've read the book must have some significance... right?

At the very least, it had increased his curiosity about the book. He thought back to what they had said: the blonde telling him that Chapter Three was "soooo, well, you know!" But he hadn't read it—instead, he jumped to the end. The two officers had only asked him whether he'd read the fourth chapter—they didn't provide any clues as to what it was about. On balance, none of them had given him any useful information about the book. Except that they had read it— whatever it was they had read...

"Okay, I give up—why were they singled out?"

Who said they were singled out?

"*You* said. You just told me that they were singled out!"

We told you that they might have been singled out. Maybe, maybe not.

"So *who* was singled out, damn it!"

No one. No one was singled out. We're all in this together.

Jack remembered an old comedy album he'd once heard, titled "I Think We're All Bozos On This Bus." So maybe that's what it boiled down to...

This isn't a joke. Four hours ago you came within a hair of sucking on a pair of trouser snakes.

There was no way he would have done that. He really would have preferred to be beaten to a pulp by those two knuckle-draggers...

Four hours!

Jack jumped off the bed and ran to the small barred window in the cell door, peering out into the holding cell area. Straining, he could barely make out the clock on the far wall:

5:45

Crap. One hour and thirty-five minutes to departure. There isn't any way I can make it now...

The sound of clanging bars suddenly reverberated through the cellblock, followed by two pairs of footsteps approaching Jack's cell. Seconds later the cell door slid open, revealing a deputy and a man in a gray flannel suit.

"Good morning, Mr. Albright," said the man in the suit. "My name is Amelius Bunting, and I am serving as your court-appointed attorney. I am pleased to inform you that all charges pertaining to this incident have been dropped and that you are free to go. The deputy will escort you to the receiving area where you may collect your belongings."

Several minutes later, after signing what seemed like a ream of forms, Jack stood outside the jail trying to figure out how to get a cab to the airport. He had no idea how far away the airport was, or how long the drive would take. He had no idea where he was, period.

He reached into his carry-on, pulled out the book and opened it to the last page he had read, thinking:

Can you please tell me where on Earth I am?

Look up.

A bit theatrical, but if it helps me get to the airport…

He looked heavenward at the reddish-tinged clouds nestled in the cobalt blue sky of dawn, spread out his arms and said:

"Oh, Blessed Book of Wonders, please tell me where I am!"

He looked back down at the book.

Not up at the sky, idiot. Look up at the building.

Jack looked up at the jail. A sign over the entrance said:

GALENA COUNTY SHERIFF STATION NO. 3

His Blackberry fortunately still had a charge. After several attempts, he was able to reach Directory Information and from there the number for the local cab company.

Fifteen minutes to wait—another eternity.

He reopened the book, finding himself at the next chapter:

Chapter Five
Conquering Your Fears

There comes a time when choices need to be made. Actually, there are innumerable circum-

stances when choices are made, as we've already illustrated—but on occasion these choices require quick thinking in critical situations. In such instances, instinct kicks in. This is fine and good, especially when self-preservation is at stake, but advance preparation will help to channel your energies and clarify your course of action.

"You mean, like when I screamed."

No. You had no advance preparation in handling that situation. You fantasized about yanking their johnsons and then performing some sort of amazing kung fu move on the two of them. Both of those men were well over six feet tall, two hundred fifty pounds apiece, with lots of experience handling twerps much quicker and nastier than you. What do you think would have happened if you had tried to follow through on your plan?

"No idea, but I'm sure you're going to tell me."

Oh, we're certain that you know full well what would have happened. You just don't want to think about it. That's okay—it's not a pleasant thought.

"So you're telling me that you saved my ass in there."

Crudely phrased, albeit applicable.

"I guess I owe you one."

You don't owe us anything. All we did was suggest that you jump ahead to the last part of your plan. Screaming was the final stage of your escapade, right?

"Well, yeah, it was…"

So it was your plan all along. We just edited out the superfluous.

"The part that would have gotten me killed, you mean."

Enough on that. Turn the page.

Jack turned the page.

As we were saying, there are times when choices need to be made, and some of these can be extremely important—perhaps matters of life and death. Decisions must be arrived at very quickly without the type of lengthy research, analysis and weighing of the pros and cons that you're accustomed to. In fact, reaction must be on a subconscious level—gut instinct, if you will.

Why are they telling me this? Jack wondered.

The better conditioned you are in advance, both physically and mentally, the better prepared you'll be and more likely to respond effectively.

"So, what do you want me to do?"

You were sitting on that bunk bed in the cell for hours. Why don't you do some stretching exercises to limber up a bit—get the blood flowing to your extremities and loosen up your muscles.

"Um... okay. Any specific exercises you'd like to suggest?"

Do some neck rolls, shoulder and arm rotations, waist twists, deep knee bends, calf stretches and ankle flexes—the basic drill.

Jack placed the book on the pavement and did some warm-up exercises, starting with his neck and continuing down through his feet, then working back up through his body. He wondered what he must look like, standing out in front of a police station at the break of dawn doing calisthenics—but considering what had already happened to him, he no longer cared. He did three full sets, then picked the book back up.

How are you feeling?

"Better, actually. Especially considering that I haven't gotten any sleep or anything to eat."

People can go without sleep for a couple of days without feeling any serious physical effects. And you actually microslept while you waited for your food at the club and when you were reading on the bunk in the cell. Some people call it daydreaming or "zoning out", but it's actually a short sleeping spell. You had quite a few of them. As for eating, it won't hurt you to lose a few pounds.

"I'm not fat!"

We didn't say you were fat. We said it wouldn't hurt you to lose a few pounds. Anyway, enough of this—your cab is only a couple of blocks away. You've limbered up slightly—that's good. Now you need to exercise your brain, loosen up your mind. In the cab, look around you. Observe things.

"What am I looking for?"

Nothing in particular—just try to pay attention. Make it a kind of game. See how many things you can notice during the trip.

Jack shrugged. "Okay, I can do that."

Good boy. Maybe you'll learn something and not even realize it.

Did they always have to be so patronizing?

He tucked the book into his carry-on as the cab pulled up in front of the sheriff's station.

The driver rolled down his window. "Dispatcher said you want the airport, that right?"

"Yes," Jack nodded, getting into the cab, "How long?"

"Forty minutes or thereabouts. You in a hurry?"

"Yes! Big tip in it if you make it faster."

"Hey, Buddy, I ain't breakin' no laws gettin' you there, but I'll see what I can do. Money is a big incentive for me."

Jack checked his pockets and billfold, counting twenty-two

dollars. He leaned toward the cab driver. "How much to the airport?"

"Pro'lly 'bout thirty bucks, plus that fat tip you promised."

"Do you take credit cards?"

The driver turned around and gave him a scornful look. "Does this look like Los Angeles?"

"Where's the closest ATM?"

"There's one on the way—I thought you was in a hurry."

"You want to get paid, right? ATM first, but quickly, please!"

As the taxi traveled through the small town, Jack remembered the book's instructions and watched out his window, observing the houses, stores and streets passing by.

What am I supposed to be looking for? No idea—just look.

The back of a stop sign caught his eye as it traveled past from left to right. A silvery octagon.

Is that significant? Does it mean something?

There was a homeless person sitting on a stoop in front of a brick house, holding a bottle. Jack tried to see what type—beer, booze, soda—but the man and the bottle traveled out of sight.

A drugstore passed by with an old red neon NEHI sign lit in the window, the neon flickering from age. Next to the stuttering NEHI was another old neon sign for beef jerky with only JERK lit.

There was a young man out walking his dog. The dog had its leg raised, peeing on a fire hydrant.

They traveled by a storm drain with a manhole cover.

After that came a building with stately columns: First National Bank.

"Hey, we just passed a bank! I told you I needed an ATM

machine!"

The driver turned halfway around. "No ATM at that bank and they're closed… it's six-twenty in the mornin', for cryin' out loud. You want me to stop at every bank you see?"

"No, sorry," Jack said, sitting back in his seat and looking out the window again.

A house with a bright blue door passed by.

Really ugly color for a door.

Then another fire hydrant.

There was a low brick wall. As it traveled by, the top edge seemed to undulate, revealing the unevenness of its cement cap.

An old painted advertising mural on the side of a brick building came into view: "Get a Leg Up on the Competition". Jack had no idea what the product was.

There was another homeless person: an old lady pulling a small two-wheeled cart filled with trash.

Maybe it just looks like trash—probably her sole possessions.

Then a glimpse of a large black cat sitting on the sidewalk licking its privates.

Right after that, another storm drain.

Then another hydrant.

What the hell am I supposed to be looking for?

There was a partially-torn billboard in a vacant lot with a big red X over a cigarette and the slogan: "Kick the Habit!"

Anti-smoking campaign… or maybe an ad for a nicotine patch?

They passed by a house with a small porch and a white wooden bench swing in need of a paint job.

Then a blue postal collection box.

Then a tan pickup truck parked at the curb with an old McCain/Palin bumper sticker plastered on the back window, followed by a sporting goods store with a poster in its display window of a man palming a basketball.

Next to the sporting goods was a music store featuring a large advertisement for a Smash Mouth CD.

Then something that looked like old red paint splattered on the sidewalk.

Yet another indigent ambling along the street—an African American with his hands shoved in his pockets. Jack had never realized there were so many homeless people.

A fourth fire hydrant. He suddenly noticed that he was keeping count.

After that, a 7-Eleven with an ATM machine outside.

The cab driver pulled up to the curb. Jack hopped out of the taxi and ran up to the ATM, inserted his charge card and typed in his PIN number, then "200" and tapped ENTER. The machine hummed for a moment, then dispensed the cash. As he reached for the small stack of bills, he felt the painful prick of a sharp object poking him in the back, just beneath his ribcage.

"Yo' money, honky!"

Several thoughts raced through Jack's head: losing the money... missing his flight... being stabbed outside a 7-Eleven in the middle of nowhere...

He turned around to face the mugger and realized it was the last homeless person he saw—or that he had assumed was homeless. He was surprised by how much the man resembled the president—then chastised himself for thinking such a thought.

Is it just because this asshole's black? His buzz cut closely resembles Obama's, and his ears kind of stick out the same way, and his eyebrows and lips...

"What you lookin' at, mo'fo'?" demanded the man clutching the knife. He appeared very nervous. "Gimme yo' goddamn money, *now!*"

Jack's own heart was pounding. His thoughts suddenly narrowed to two: fight or flight.

He had voted for McCain.

His right knee jerked up impulsively, violently, into the black man's crotch. Caught by surprise, the attacker doubled over in agony, and Jack shifted his weight, grabbing the back of the man's head with his left hand and bringing his left knee up into the assailant's face. Blood spurted out of the robber's nose as he collapsed on the ground.

Jack ran to the cab and jumped into the back seat, yelling: "Let's go!"

As the driver gunned the engine, he glanced back at Jack. "Nice move back there."

"Yeah, thanks. I have no idea where that came from."

The cab driver managed to exceed the speed limit on the way to the airport—not nearly as fast as the previous night's ride in the blonde's Camaro, but still a good pace—arriving at five before seven. Jack flung sixty dollars into the front of the cab and jumped out, racing into the terminal.

Twenty-five minutes to go. Plenty of time.

Then he remembered airport security.

"Please get in line and have your boarding pass ready to present to the security officer," a uniformed woman intoned.

Jack got into the shortest line.

"Do you have a Priority One Fast Pass?" The uniformed woman inquired.

"Um, no."

"Do you have an Executive Preferred Expedite Card?"

"No, no I don't."

"Then please move over to the Passenger Express line."

Jack joined the end of the longest line.

Ten minutes later, he was halfway to the security screener's stand.

He pulled out the book and turned to where he had left off.

> Security at the nation's airports was significantly enhanced in the aftermath of the terrorist attacks on September 11, 2001. Newly instituted changes included prohibitions on carrying any knives or potential weapons into secured airport areas or onto airplanes as defined by the FAA under its Hazardous Materials Guidelines. In 2006, additional restrictions were imposed on passengers carrying more than three ounces of any gels, liquids or aerosols. All bottles and other liquid-carrying items had to be presented to security screeners in a single clear plastic bag not exceeding one-quart capacity.
>
> In addition, airplane passengers must present their boarding pass and valid state or federal government-issued identification to security personnel, must remove their shoes for inspection, must pass through metal detectors and other detection devices and are subject to searches, including full-body searches.
>
> Persons who have recently been arrested and/or incarcerated are subject to additional screening

measures, as specified by federal and local law en-
forcement regulations.

Why are they telling me this?

He carefully reread it, trying to find some hidden clue.

"Your boarding pass and driver's license, sir," the white-
gloved screener demanded.

Jack glanced up from the book and realized that he was at
the front of the line. He reached into his jacket pocket, pulled
out his boarding pass and handed it to the uniformed man,
then took out his wallet, removed his driver's license and
handed that to the man as well.

"Please have these ready to hand to the security agent the
next time you travel in order to avoid unnecessary delays," the
screener intoned as he looked over Jack's pass and license. He
looked up at Jack, studying him, then back down at the license
and pass, then back up at Jack, then back down at the documents. "Your flight is scheduled to depart in five minutes."

"Yes, yes, I know," Jack replied, as nonchalantly as he
could manage.

The screener handed the boarding pass and license back to
him. "Please arrive at the airport at least two hours before your
flight's scheduled departure the next time you travel in order
to allow sufficient time for your security screening," the
screener intoned. "Please proceed to the conveyor area and
place all loose items and your shoes into a conveyor tray and
follow the instructions of the screening personnel at the
conveyor area. Thank you and have a safe trip."

Jack hustled over to the conveyors and waited in that line,
yanking off his shoes and placing them and his carry-on, belt,
wallet, keys, and loose change into a tray as soon as he reached

the stack, then waited to walk through the metal detector, then hurried over to collect his items from the tray, struggling with his shoes, stuffing his belt, wallet, keys and change into his carry-on and then raced down the passageway and turned down the corridor toward the departure area, almost colliding with a returning soldier strapped to an IV in a wheel chair, shouting his apologies as he turned left down the long concourse he had waited in yesterday toward Gate... Gate...

Which gate do I need?

He frantically looked around for a departure announcement board, spying one halfway down the concourse and running over to it.

Which flight?

He pulled the boarding pass out of his jacket pocket and scanned it for the flight number.

Flight 903.

He looked back up at the board—

Flight	Dest	Departs	Status	Gate
903	CHI	7:20am	Boarding	D17

Wrong corridor.

He ran back along the hallway to the end, looking for a sign to the D gates.

To the right and down the escalator.

He hurried to the escalator, took the steps by twos, turned right again and rushed down the concourse.

D17 was at the end.

D3... D5... D7... D9... D11... D13... D15...

Up ahead!

The door was closed.

Jack ran over to a woman dressed in an Occidental Airways uniform who was standing near the door.

"That's my flight!"

The agent shook her head and gave him a sympathetic look. "I'm sorry, sir, but it's already leaving the gate."

Jack glanced out the window and saw the nose of the plane beginning to edge away from the boarding causeway.

Crap.

He watched it slowly glide backward until the nose disappeared from view.

Crap. Crap. Crap.

He turned away from the window.

Ah, well. No use crying over it.

He slowly walked over to the reception desk. There wasn't any line. He booked the next available flight at 9:50am, and then went in search of a cup of coffee with something to slake his gnawing hunger.

Seated at a small table, halfway through his coffee and bran muffin, he reached into his carry-on for the book.

He felt around for it.

He looked down at the bag.

No book. Where was the book?

His mind raced back, trying to retrace his steps.

When did I have it last? Waiting in line at the security check-in, reading about the new security measures.

He gulped down the remainder of his coffee, stuffed the rest of the muffin into his mouth and walked back through the airport to the security area. He found a guard standing on the cleared-passenger side.

"Excuse me, but I've lost a book. Has anyone found a paperback called 'Learning to Swim'?"

The guard pointed down a corridor. "Lost items claim down that hallway, third door on the left."

Jack followed the guard's directions. When he reached it, the door was locked. A neatly printed sign on the door read:

Hours of Operation: 11am—5pm

Crap.

He walked back up the corridor to the guard. "It's closed."

"Hours of operation are 11am to 5pm," the guard intoned.

"I know, I saw the sign. My flight leaves before then."

The guard pointed down the same corridor. "You may file a lost items report at Airport Security Operations. Second door on the right."

"Okay, thanks."

He started down the hallway, then remembered the last thing he had read in the book: about special scrutiny of people who had recently been arrested. Maybe the book was telling him something… maybe it was better not to rock the boat.

Then Jack remembered the bookstore—about returning there last night and picking up another copy of "Learning to Swim", and how it was just like his version at the point where he had left off.

He traversed the airport until he reached the concourse with the bookstore and proceeded to the paperback rack. He quickly scanned the book spines and covers from top to bottom, turning the carousel one full rotation.

No more copies.

He went through the rack again: nothing.

He walked over to the clerk at the counter: a young fellow with a Vandyke moustache and goatee.

"May I help you?" the clerk asked.

"Yes, I'm looking for a paperback novel titled 'Learning to Swim.' You had several copies on the rack over there yesterday."

The clerk shook his head. "Sorry, I'm not familiar with that title. You said we had several copies?"

"Yes, just yesterday."

The clerk shook his head again. "Sometimes copies get buried toward the back. Did you check the entire rack?"

"Yes, twice. No copies left. Could you have any in the back?"

The clerk shook his head a third time. "Sorry, everything we have is out on the floor. If it's not there, I'm afraid we're sold out."

"Okay, thanks."

He walked back over to the rack.

Why did it have to be "Learning to Swim"? They could modify any book they wanted to—it could be Webster's Dictionary for all it mattered.

He picked up another novel and flipped through it.

Normal.

Another one.

Nothing special.

He scanned through several others, then gave up.

He left the store, walking back through the airport to the D Gates concourse. Still thirsty, he purchased a second cup of coffee at one of the eateries and slowly drank it, then found a restroom and freshened up as best he could. He continued down the concourse to the D17 waiting area, found a seat and looked at his watch:

8:30. An hour and twenty minutes to go.

He felt lost without the book. It was a profound sense of loss—like some vital appendage had been surgically removed.

How could I have been so careless? That mad dash to the gate trying to make the plane—for what?

A large flat screen TV monitor on the wall caught his eye. In truth, it was the crowd beginning to form around the TV that drew his attention. They were watching what looked like a news report.

He stood and walked over toward the monitor. The image on screen was an airport. It looked just like the airport he was standing in. The title at the bottom of the picture read:

SPECIAL REPORT: DISASTER IN THE AIR

Jack moved closer in order to hear the announcer.

"… just a few moments ago. We're still getting up-to-the-minute details from FAA, but it appears that Occidental Airways Flight 903 en route to Chicago has crashed some-where in the mountains west of Denver. Skies are clear and weather does not seem to have been a factor. Again, details are sketchy at this point, but initial reports are that air traffic controllers lost contact with the airplane as it was crossing over the Rocky Mountains in Colorado. There are no reports of casualties at this time, but another aircraft in the vicinity has reported seeing a large plume of smoke in the area where the plane is feared to have gone down. Again, Occidental Airways Flight 903 en route to O'Hare International Airport in Chicago is reported to have crashed somewhere west of Denver, Colorado."

Jack watched along with the other passengers, transfixed.

Immediately after the news bulletin, he called home to tell

Helen that he hadn't taken the flight. She wondered whether he should cancel his 9:50 departure. Jack wondered the same thing, but decided that the accident had no bearing on future flights—in fact, a sort of perverse statistical logic took hold: the chances of a second accident happening to the same airline company on the same route on the same day had to be infinitesimal.

The hours that followed seemed like a dream to Jack, a slow-motion trance. There were constant news reports detailing facts and rumors—sightings, suppositions, and speculation: Mechanical malfunction? Pilot error? Terrorist attack? There was a steady stream of interviews with disaster response experts explaining rescue procedures; FAA officials detailing the agency's actions; politicians grabbing airtime to demand an investigation; and Occidental Airways spokesmen expressing remorse while cautioning against rash judgments.

His 9:50 flight to Chicago was delayed for more than an hour, finally departing at 11:05. It was only half-full: considering what had happened to the previous flight, Jack was hardly surprised. Like everyone else on the plane, his eyes were glued to the seven-inch LCD screen in the back of the seat facing him. An hour into his journey home came the awful news: no survivors.

When he reached O'Hare and turned his Blackberry back on, he saw that there were several cell phone calls from Lacey, his secretary. After purchasing the half-dozen roses for Helen and some candy for the kids to make up for the lost toys, Jack called Lacey back on his way to his car.

"Jack? I've been trying to reach you all afternoon, we've been worried stiff!" Lacey said. "I finally called your house and talked to your wife—she told us you were taking a later flight. Oh, thank God! Why didn't you fly home yesterday? Where are you?"

"I just landed at O'Hare. It's a long story. What are you doing at work on Saturday?"

"I'm not at work, I'm at home," she said. "We were worried you also took that morning flight. Jack... do you know about Nick Hargrove?" Lacey's voice was breaking.

"No, what about Nick?" He knew before she replied.

"Jack, he was on that plane. The one that went down." She was crying. "Jack... Nick's dead."

"Oh, dear God, no," Jack said, stopping short in the middle of the parking lot.

Of course Nick would be on that plane—he always stayed overnight and took the first flight out the next day. Part of his modus operandi. His modus operandi... was it wrong to talk that way about someone who had just died?

"I was scheduled to take that flight, too."

Lacey was sniffling now. "Well, thank goodness you didn't. Why didn't you?"

"Long story," Jack said, resuming his walk.

"Mr. Sunderland wants to have a special meeting this evening at headquarters. Can you make it?"

George Sunderland was CEO of GlobalReach.

"Of course. What time?"

"Six o'clock. He'll have dinner brought in. It's the Executive Staff, but he asked for you, too."

Why me? Maybe because I knew Nick fairly well? Or because we'd both gone on this trip? Would they ask me to give an account of the trip? If so, would it be limited to the meeting portion, or would they want to know about the entire trip?

He instinctively reached into his carry-on.

Crap.

He really missed that damn book.

He arrived home at 4:55pm and had just enough time to greet his wife and children, then quickly shave, shower and change before he drove to the office.

The corporate headquarters of GlobalReach was a twelve-story, glass-and-concrete monolith, virtually indistinguishable from the scores of other large business offices in the Chicago suburbs. As with most headquarters buildings, the uppermost story housed the CEO's offices and the boardroom. A brick-paved circular drive leading to the entrance wrapped around a mini-park with landscaped trees and wooden benches. A huge wire-frame globe dominated the center of the park, mounted atop a ten-foot stainless steel pedestal: the GlobalReach logo. The globe was painted blue and tan to signify the oceans and continents, with GLOBAL in green letters spanning the northern hemisphere, and REACH in red letters curving the bottom.

Jack took the executive elevator to the twelfth floor, the doors opening onto a vestibule lined with portraits of the board of directors. A pair of large glass doors at the end of the antechamber led to the Executive Suite. Approaching the entrance, Jack noticed that an easel positioned just inside held a large, ornately-gilded frame with a recent photograph of Nick, the frame draped in black cloth. A second easel held a foam board with professional lettering that read:

Nick Hargrove
Senior Vice President of Marketing

1966 - 2010

Impressive job by Internal Communications on such short notice, Jack thought, *and on a Saturday, too.*

He wondered whether they had photos of every Senior Vice President prepped for this kind of situation, and how far down the corporate ladder these kinds of preparations went...

Milling around the reception area beyond the easels were all of the top brass at GlobalReach; each man holding a mixed drink and engaged in conversation. Donald Shabbersham, Senior Vice President of Accounting, saw Jack through the doors and motioned for him to enter.

"Terrible news, Jack, isn't it?" Don greeted him. "Thank God you weren't on that plane, too. We were talking about Nick, remembering some of the things he used to do. Get yourself a drink."

Jack walked over to the wet bar and asked the bartender for a scotch on the rocks. No need to specify brand—it was always Glenlivet 21-Year Single Malt. GlobalReach only stocked the best for its executive staff and board members. Jack was still developing an affinity for scotch—he actually pre-ferred blended whiskeys—but he knew that he had to wean himself from such lower-class tastes if he expected to climb the corporate ladder. Besides, at one hundred dollars per bottle, he couldn't afford twenty-one-year-old single malt scotch: this was a rare luxury.

He rejoined Don's group, nodding and smiling at the little anecdotes each man offered about Nick. Eventually, it was his turn to share.

"You were with him out west, Jack," Guy Forester, Senior Vice President of Administrative Services observed. "By the way, we heard about the bang-up job you did out there, landing that contract with Bradlee Brothers—congratulations! Did Nick say anything to you in particular, anything you'd like to share?"

Yes, actually, he did. He suggested that we both head out to a strip club in the middle of nowhere, and although I declined his offer, I ended up there anyway and I got a lap dance by some whore until the place got busted and I ended up in a jail cell with two inbred mutants who planned to rape me until I screamed like a teenage girl in a slasher movie and I was released and went to an ATM machine to get cash for a cab ride where I was mugged by a black guy with a knife who looked a lot like Obama, but I somehow managed to knee him in the balls and then I bloodied his face and I raced to the airport and barely missed the plane that Nick was on.

"No, nothing really," Jack said instead. "We spoke for a moment after the meeting. It's incredible—I mean, I was talking to him just yesterday, and now he's gone. He was a really great guy."

"Yeah," the other men nodded in agreement. "A great guy." They sipped their Glenlivets.

Soon after, they were ushered into the boardroom. They seated themselves around the mammoth horseshoe-shaped table and George Sunderland walked over to the podium.

"Good evening, gentlemen, and lady," he began, nodding to the only woman present: Virginia Kempler, Senior Vice President of Internal Communications, was the token female executive staff member. She politely nodded back, acknowledging her special status.

"You all know why we are gathered here tonight on this most unfortunate occasion," Sunderland continued. "We are here to pay tribute to our Senior Vice President of Marketing,

Nick Hargrove, who passed away earlier today. I would like to ask John Peabody to lead us in a prayer for Nick. John, if you would be so kind…"

John Peabody was Senior Vice President of Operations. In his previous vocation he had been the pastor of a small Methodist church, and he served as the de facto deliverer of blessings, invocations and benedictions at corporate headquarters.

John stood up and bowed his head, as did everyone else around the table.

"In the name of our Savior and Lord Jesus Christ, let us pray…"

After the prayer, Sunderland gave a short speech honoring Nick, and then he enumerated the corporation's policies pertaining to the unanticipated demise of executive staff members: Press releases would be prepared for release on Monday morning. Once funeral arrangements had been made, all employees who wished to attend would be granted liberal leave. Any employee requiring counseling should be referred to the Human Resources Department by their immediate supervisor. He concluded by mentioning that Virginia would include a special tribute to Nick in next month's employee newsletter.

"Nice job on the commemoration in the reception area by the way, Virginia."

She gave him a demure smile and nod of thanks.

White-jacketed waiters then served dinner: it began with an appetizer of smoked Coho salmon served over melted Gruyère cheese on medallions of garlic-toasted French bread. The entrée was coq au van with shallots and mushrooms, new potatoes, carrots julienne and Parker House rolls with honey glaze. Jack had no idea what wine was served, much less its vintage, but even his untrained palate could tell that it was very good stock. Dessert consisted of fresh raspberries in a Grenadine and Cointreau triple sec sauce served over a large cream-filled white marzipan truffle.

During dessert, Sunderland walked around the table, thanking each officer for attending. When he reached Jack, he leaned over and whispered: "Please stop by my office on your way out."

Sunderland's office was a suite of rooms that included a reception area, a small kitchen, a dining room, an exercise room, a private bath with shower and two meeting rooms leading up to a mahogany-paneled library and workplace. His ornate desk reminded Jack of the one Kennedy had used in the Oval Office, which John-John played under in the famous picture. Sunderland was busy on the phone—he motioned Jack in, pointing to one of the seats across from the mammoth desk.

"… we need to move things along on that, wouldn't you agree?" Sunderland was saying into his wireless headset. "I have complete confidence in you, Jerry. Yes, yes, I know that. Just make it work and do it quickly. Don't worry about the details—I'll have Pat up in legal wrestle with the small print… you just make sure they sign by Tuesday. Okay. Okay then. Okay, nice talking to you, Jerry, bye." He lifted off the earphone and turned to Jack.

"No rest for the weary, Jack. Thanks for coming out here tonight. I know you just got back in and you haven't had time to be with your family." Sunderland shook his head, frowning. "Terrible thing that happened to Nick. You know, I'm the one who brought Nick on board. It was October 2001—I remember because it was right after 9-11. Our first vice president of marketing was a guy by the name of Lansdowne—Harry Lansdowne. He was at the twin towers that day, meeting with some of our underwriters. Another terrible tragedy. That was a few years before you came on board, so you probably didn't know about that. Harry was a great guy—he helped get this company underway. He was a pro when it came to handling startup businesses like ours—finding investment bankers, raising venture capital, issuing IPOs—that kind of thing. He didn't know squat about marketing to the Feds, though.

"Anyway, we had to find a replacement for Harry. As you know, most of our largest federal contracts deal with security matters, and we had to move quickly to grab these. The handwriting was on the wall—there was talk of a new Homeland Security Agency or Department and, well, opportunity was knocking and I wanted to make sure we got a good slice of the pie."

He leaned back in his chair, playing with a pen.

"I knew that Nick was the guy to do it. He came from the Feds—I don't know if you were aware of that. He had a solid background in handling government bids, and he knew how to hurdle all the regulations and procedures. Plus, he knew folks on the inside—he was on a first-name basis with some of the key decision-makers. And it all worked out just like..." his voice trailed off momentarily. "...just like we knew it would. During the past decade, GlobalReach has grown tenfold. We're a big player now, thanks in no small part to Nick. His loss leaves us with some pretty big shoes to fill."

Sunderland stopped playing with the pen and leaned forward.

"But it also provides us with an opportunity. Nick's role was to land these fat federal grants, and he accomplished that better than anyone else. Now that we have those contracts, our mission has changed. We need to hold onto them, tightly, and not give the feds any reason to look elsewhere. The maxim back then was 'rapid responsiveness and innovation'—good stuff, but times change. The watchwords today are 'efficiency and accountability'. We've got government bean counters breathing down our necks, demanding constant assurances that their precious taxpayer dollars aren't being wasted. GlobalReach needs to change gears—we need to reposition ourselves as trustworthy, effective, safe and reliable."

He looked squarely at Jack. "That's where you come in."

"Me, sir?"

"Your presentation yesterday convinced the Board that you have what it takes, Jack. You know how things work: you know the ins and outs of our business and you know how to get the biggest bang for the buck. You're a CPA with an MBA from Wharton, for Christ's sake! You know how to check the ledgers and make sure that everything is being done above board, while at the same time maximizing return. And most importantly," he pointed with his pen to emphasize each word, "you know how to communicate this to others. You might be a bean counter by trade, but you're also a natural born salesman, Jack. You know how to make an airtight case and sell it to the client. The days of bells and whistles and candy-coated promises are over, Jack—the new business model is parsimonious, penny-pinching professionalism. And you, Jack Albright, reek of that!"

Sunderland stood up and offered his hand.

"I'm offering you the position of Senior Vice President of Marketing at GlobalReach, Jack. It's up to you, of course, but I'd think you'd be a damn fool to turn it down!"

Jack stood and shook Sunderland's hand.

"I… I don't know what to say."

"How about: 'Thanks, Mr. Sunderland, I'm your man!'"

"Yes, thanks Mr. Sunderland. I'm your man, sir! I really am deeply honored to be offered the position!"

"Good! I'm glad that's the way you feel—I know you'll do us proud."

Sunderland patted his own stomach. "That Pinot Blanc went right through me. If you'll excuse me for a moment, Jack, I need to provide it an outlet, so to speak. We'll go over some details when I get back."

Sunderland walked out of his office toward his private bath.

Already standing, Jack wandered over to the adjacent library. His head was swimming.

Senior Vice President! Of marketing… what the heck do I know about marketing? Then again, what the heck does any senior vice president know about anything? Forester doesn't know anything about administrative services—he's got a psych degree and started out in human resources. Peabody, head of operations, was an ex-pastor, for Christ's sake. What was Nick's background? Like Sunderland mentioned, he came from the feds—but all he did over there was contracts. No marketing experience to speak of…

Jack had only been in Sunderland's office a few times over the years, always passing through the library but never having the opportunity to stop to take a closer look. As he scanned the books neatly stacked on the shelves, one caught his eye—it was a hardbound copy while his had been a paperback, but the spine was unmistakable. He took it down from the shelf and looked at the cover:

Learning to Swim

He gingerly opened the book and turned over the flyleaf to the title page.

Learning to Swim
A Novel of Our Times

By James J. Anderson

2010
MacHall Press / New York

A Subsidiary of GlobalReach Enterprises

Jack heard the dull whooshing sound of a flushing toilet. He hurriedly shelved the book and returned to his chair. A moment later, Sunderland came back into the office.

"Ah, much better! When you get to be my age, you'll appreciate the finer points of life, Jack—like a restroom within easy walking distance."

He sat down in his desk chair.

"On Monday, come into work and report to accounting as usual. During the morning executive meeting, I'll have you come in, and at that time I'll make the announcement about your new position. Some folks around the company, especially in marketing, may be taking news of Nick's misfortune rather hard... so we'll hold up on announcing your appointment company-wide for a few days. That will give you time to meet with some of the key folks to help get you acclimated." Sunderland rolled his eyes. "God knows with the rumor mills around here, everyone will know within minutes anyway, but I'll arrange a meeting of the Marketing Department late Friday and introduce you there, to make it formal. Any questions?"

Jack shook his head no.

"Okay then…" Sunderland stood, came around his desk and shook Jack's hand once more, giving him a slap on the back. "It's been a trying day for all of us. Get yourself home and get some rest, and I'll see you Monday morning."

On the drive home, Jack made a mental note to bring more cash on his next business trip, and to rent a car.

And he prayed that the federal government would continue to insist on parsimonious professionalism until he reached retirement.

❧

Dead in Mt. Isa

By David W. Brooks

The old man had looked a lot like Popeye when alive, but now that he was dead the resemblance was uncanny. He lay on his side against the faded flowers of the couch, giving Raymond a good view of the plump cheeks, hooked nose and slit-like eyes that spelled The Sailor Man to anybody who grew up in front of an American television set. Only the blue skin spoiled the effect, but then the color TV in Raymond's basement had always been a bit off, so he was used to that.

He went into the kitchen where the Swede was eating a sandwich and said, "I think Charlie's dead." The Swede only scoffed. "No, really, I mean it. I went in and he was sitting hunched over on the couch and he didn't say anything, so I went up to him and touched him on the shoulder and he just slumped over on his side and lay there. Really." The Swede, who had blue eyes and blonde hair and a scruffy half-dark beard and looked exactly like the sailor he had been before he jumped ship in Perth, gave Raymond a look of pity. "Sure Charlie is dead," he said in his stereotyped accent. "Just like you are a Canadian newspaper reporter, huh?"

"I was just kidding then—this is serious. I think he's really dead. Go take a look." But two days of practical jokes had taken their toll on the Swede. "Sure, we go in, and Charlie his is standing there and you both laugh at me. Thank you very much, no. I will rather eat here in quiet." Raymond was flustered; they couldn't just sit and have breakfast while their host lay blue and silent ten feet away. "Really, I'm not kidding this time, honest," he pleaded, but a hint of a smile had snuck into his voice and a twitch had appeared at the corner of his mouth; why, he didn't know. He tried again: "It's true, he's really dead," and found himself bursting into a gulp of laughter as he spoke. It was as if his mind could not take death, which it had never seen before, seriously.

The Swede, busy with his sandwich, was no longer paying any attention. Raymond thought of dragging him into the living room but feared it would turn into a wrestling match on the kitchen floor. Then he thought of dragging Charlie into the kitchen and displaying him as proof, but that didn't seem quite right. If they had a Polaroid camera he could take a picture and show it; the look of death was unmistakable. But they didn't have the camera.

Then he got an idea. "Look, I'll tell you what. You go in and look at him, and if he isn't dead I'll give you ten dollars. Ten *American* dollars." This made the Swede stop chewing: the joke was turning out to be more complicated than it appeared. "You give me ten dollars if Charlie is alive?"

"Right. Here it is." Raymond opened his wallet and pulled out the bill. The Swede came forward and examined it; he always thought it a great drawback that you cannot tell the amount on American money from a distance. He stared at Raymond. "And what if Charlie is dead, what then?"

"Then we call the hospital, I guess."

"But I do not give you ten dollars?"

"No. It's not a bet. I just want you to look at him."

The Swede sat back in his chair and meditatively picked

crumbs off his plate. He couldn't figure it out. This *had* to be a joke; there had been almost nothing but jokes between him and Raymond since Charlie had brought the American back from the bar two days earlier: false names, imaginary backgrounds, prickly burrs in each other's beds—nothing malicious, not like the freighter, where they laughed when you burned the skin off your arm, but nothing solemn either. To lure him into an unnecessary trip to the living room with such a flimsy story as a sudden death would be a big victory for Raymond and he would never hear the end of it. But even so, wasn't that worth ten dollars? Even if there was a trip wire waiting for him or a bucket of water balanced on the door, wasn't that worth ten dollars? Wouldn't it take the sting out of any victory when Raymond had to hand over the green bill with the strange man on it? He decided that it would. "Okay, I will go look," he said, and with infinite caution he inched down the hall, past the crusted cans of paint and the irregular piles of boards to the living room, where he carefully opened the door with the toe of his boot and stepped inside. An instant later he was back out again, astonished.

"My God, you are not making a joke: Charlie *is* dead!" He rushed past Raymond to the corner of the kitchen where his sleeping bag lay and pulled out a pack of cigarettes. "What do we do," he asked, lighting up.

"I guess we go to the hospital."

The Swede puffed furiously. "Yes, the hospital. Perhaps he is not all the way dead. You know where it is?" Raymond nodded; the hospital, perhaps the largest building in the small Australian mining town, was hard to overlook. "Then you go there and tell this to them, okay?"

"Okay, I'll run over." There was no car, no bicycle, no

phone; Charlie said he preferred life unencumbered by objects, but the real reason was, of course, that he was stone broke. "I should be back in ten minutes."

"Sure, okay. Go!"

Raymond had a hard time making the nurse at the hospital believe him; he couldn't keep the smile out of his voice. "You sure he's dead?" The girl's accent was thick and sharp, like sour butter.

"I'm not positive but I think so. Somebody should come look at him—I mean, his face is all blue." She stared at him, suspicious. "And you don't even know his last name?"

"No, I only just met him. I'm just staying there for a couple days on my way through. I'm an American."

"Never would have guessed. All right; where is he then?"

"I don't know the address, but it's a beat-up white house on the edge of the parking lot opposite Bailey's Hardware Store. About three blocks that way." He pointed through a wall and the nurse brightened.

"Oh, I know who you mean—the old feller who paints signs!"

"Yeah, that's him. The house is full of them."

"He's dead? Too bad." She picked up a phone and barked instructions. "Ambulance'll be there right off," she told him. "The police'll be by, too. Better get back."

When he returned the Swede was gone. There was no sign that he had ever been in the house, not a cigarette butt or a book of matches, not a piece of clothing, not a note. Raymond was surprised to find that he was not surprised. The Swede had been leery of the police out of fear of immigration officials, so it made sense that he didn't want to be associated with a sudden death. The only problem was what to tell the police.

But the police didn't care. They came with the ambulance and a young officer questioned Raymond for a few minutes, making occasional notes in a black booklet. Raymond told him how he was travelling around Australia and how he had gone into the Miner's Bar after getting off the bus in Mt. Isa and met Charlie there. "He was the only one around so we got to talking and when I asked him about hotels he invited me to come back here. So I did."

The officer gave him a glance. "I'd be a bit suspicious, meself, of an old man who invited young fellers to come sleep at his house."

Raymond flushed. "I thought of that, of course, but I knew I could always leave. It's not like he could overpower me or anything; he was pretty old."

"A bit of a pisser, ai."

"Yes, he was drunk a lot of the time. But he was a nice guy, and when you're travelling it's good to meet the local people, so I stayed here. He gave me a bed in the front room."

"And this was Tuesday you said? So what have you done since then?"

"Oh, tourist stuff, you know. Looking around. I rented a moke yesterday and we all—he and I—went driving into the bush. We saw some emus."

"And he seemed all right to you? Not like he was about to pop off?"

"All right for a guy his age, yes. He complained that he couldn't sleep and that his stomach bothered him. And he's been having these itches lately…"

"Have a few itches meself." The policeman laughed at his own joke and closed his book. "Everything seems clear enough. Must have given you a bit of a shock when you found him in there," he suggested, in a conversational tone. "Yes," Raymond answered, although he wasn't sure that it had.

The policeman, looking around the room, hardly listened. "Don't see why you want to stay in a dump like this," he muttered, "Bloody house looks like it's about to fall over."

They were sitting on the sofa where Charlie had died and lay stiffening until the corpsman took him away; the officer pounded on a plywood wall with his fist and made a face.

"It's free," Raymond explained. "I just had to buy a meal or two each day. And, as I said, Charlie was a nice guy. He told me a lot about Mt. Isa."

"Huh—fat lot there is to tell. Bet she seems a pretty scruffy bit of a town to you, ai?"

"No, no—it's, um, interesting. And everybody's very friendly."

"Interesting!" He snorted. "If it wasn't for the missus I'd leave, go to the coast: Brisbane, maybe Sidney. Naw, there's not much here. You've seen the mine? Of course you've seen the bloody mine; what else is there in Mt. Isa? Did you know this is the largest city in the world?" At least five people had told Raymond this; it had been the first thing Charlie had said to him after he had gotten a beer and sat on the tall wooden stool: "Hey there Yank, didja know you're in the biggest fucking city in the whole entire world?" He had been slightly drunk and ready to pick an argument but when Raymond just smiled placatingly he had switched to sudden camaraderie and soon they were talking together and drinking Raymond's beer. "No fear," said the officer, "it really is the biggest. The council pushed the boundaries right out into the bush, fifty kilometers or something every way, I dunno exactly, so we're bigger than anybody even if we have only 20,000 people and we're 300 miles from the nearest civilization. Pretty ridiculous, ai?" I guess it's for the mineral tax or something, but it seems a bit silly to me." A corpsman in a red and white jacket came and motioned at the door; the officer stood up. "Well, I guess she's done, so we'll be leaving. Enjoy your visit to 'Strylia."

"So I can leave Mt. Isa?"

"Doesn't make any difference to me, mate."

"I thought maybe I'd have to testify at an inquest or something."

"Aw, no. They'll cut 'im up back at the hospital and take a peak but it looks obvious enough: there was a bottle of Cherry Brandy and a bottle of prescription sleeping draught beside him, both empty. Looks like he drank 'em both down, maybe to get some sleep, and overloaded his system. Not unusual with these old piss-heads." He nodded a farewell and they all drove off, leaving Raymond alone in the house.

For a time he wandered through the three rooms, feeling the tingling sensation of mild trespass he had known rummaging in his parents' closet as a child, but this soon wore off. He fiddled with the old man's only possession of any value, a radio he had used to listen to Australian Rules football matches from Victoria, and poked through a pile of old magazines with their four-color pictures of celebrities and young girls in bikinis. Then he crossed the parking lot and told the news to Mr. Bailey in the hardware store.

"Dead, is he? Well, I'll be damned. I just got in and they told me an ambulance had been by. I was just going to come over..." He rubbed his head and pondered the information as Raymond watched a clerk sell a hammer to a fat man in shorts and knee-socks. "Well, he was an old bastid, no worry, so I suppose it had to come. He hit the piss awful hard, and he's seen a doctor about that stomach of his. Still, it's a bit of a shock; he's rented that house from me, oh, I suppose five years now. Must be a year behind in his rent, but nobody else'll have it in that shape and it's not worth the trouble to fix it up, so I didn't worry him much." He chuckled, then caught himself and turned somber. "Poor old bastid. I let him paint some things to help his account. He used to be good, you know. Real good with a brush, he was. Lately, though..." He shook his head. "You a relative? Oh, met him in the Miner's, did you? He'd do that occasionally, meet people passing through and put them up for a night or two. I guess he liked the company. Had this Swedish feller there recently... No, I don't think he has any family, certainly not out here. I think he came from the coast somewhere, but he's been in Isa twenty years or more now. I suppose it's up to me to put together the funeral." He looked at Raymond. "What about you? You staying at the house?" The question was friendly but there was a slight landlord ring to it.

"No, I think I'll take the evening bus out of town."

"Going east?"

"No, west. Into the interior. To Alice Springs."

"Oh, yes, Ayer's Rock and all. Very nice, that; saw it when I was a boy. Well, have a nice trip. And thanks for letting me know."

Raymond went to the bus station—a hot little building marked by a plastic sign with the long running greyhound of the company, a name and symbol developed independently of the American firm—and reserved a seat on the 6 p.m. bus that cut through the hot scrub of Queensland under cover of darkness. Then he returned to the house, where he packed up his bag and ate the last of the old man's bread and honey, telling himself that otherwise it would rot. The house was growing warm as the sun climbed in the pale blue sky. He looked out the window for a time at the tall smoke stack of the mine but eventually his attention, for lack of alternatives, turned to the house. He had been there less than three days but already a thin coat of association coated the rooms. When he looked in the corner where the Swede's bag had been—the sailor had sworn that he preferred sleeping on the floor, but Raymond suspected he just wanted to be closer to the food— he did not see the walls and floorboards but only the lack of what he was used to; when he listened to the small noises of the city he heard only the change from the noises that had been there when the old man, hacking and mumbling, had still been alive. Unconsciously he sought for things that were not differ- ent than they had been, and that brought his attention to the signs.

They were scattered throughout the house, a sort of scrap- book of a life's work, stacked and piled all over the place, the larger ones leaning against the thin plank walls that showed cracks of daylight and let in the grit of the wind, the smaller ones lying on tables and chairs and the floor. Most were wooden, although a few were painted on sheets of metal that wobbled at the touch. They ranged in size from small 'Open for Business' placards to a four-foot-square sign that said 'The Grounded Drake' in huge script with the block words 'Food' and 'Drink' and 'Darts' beneath. Raymond pulled it out of a pile with some difficulty and looked at it; it had obviously hung outdoors for many years, for the paint was faded and it was covered with dirt and fly-specks. But still he could see that it was very well done. The lettering was excellent, the lines straight and firm, the spacing perfect, the balance of the words just right. Even the little serifs at the corners of the letters were neither too large nor too small. Raymond carried it into the kitchen and propped it against the long wall, where he found that it matched exactly with marks in the wood. Obviouslty the old man had lugged it in there from time to time to admire it, and Raymond could imagine him sitting bleary-eyed in his chair, smiling on the work of his earlier years.

Most of the signs in the house were old and weather-beaten. Some were almost illegible, and some cracked or broken, but this only lent an air of dignity to their little commercial messages. As Raymond looked through them he began recognizing little tricks Charlie had used: seemingly random lines that drew attention inward; flourishes that pushed you from one word to the next. And there were certain letters he repeated from sign to sign, most notably an over-sized capital 'G' that looked very pleased with itself and a curlique lower-case 'L' that escaped the usual drabness of this most linear of letters.

The newer signs, some still with a gleam in their paint, as if Charlie had been unable to sell them, were much less impressive. In the living room a long white slab that was to say "DWIGHT'S GARAGE" sat half-finished. He could see how the old man painstakingly blocked out each letter, getting down the curves and angles in pencil before free-handing the paint, but still it was not very good; the 'W' overwhelmed the neighboring 'I' and the apostrophe hung unrelated above the word, while the two Gs in 'GARAGE" were noticeably different. Perhaps it was despair at his declining powers that had led the old man to drink down the two bottles in the night.

This was a new thought: had Charlie committed suicide? Had he deliberately downed the Cherry Brandy and the sleeping medicine in the midst of a late-night funk? Raymond didn't think this likely, for Charlie had seemed a pleasant soul, troubled by the illnesses of age and poverty but happy enough as long as he could complain a bit. But who can say what hits a man alone in the dark? *It's not like I knew him all that well— although I was the first to see him dead. And, come to think of it, the last to see him alive.* He ran through the previous night in his mind. After darkness had fallen they had sat around the little kitchen table, eating bologna and listening to the Australian Broadcast Company's top-20 show while the Swede told stories, most of them probably lies, about life on a Liberian freighter and Charlie talked about the outback before the war, when there were still camel trains carrying supplies to the center and few short-wave radios were available to break up the emptiness. Then they had gone to bed: the Swede on the kitchen floor, Charlie on the hide-a-bed, Raymond on the sagging mattress in the front room. He had looked in the living room and said 'good night' as he went; the old man, still in his long coat and red cap with frayed earmuffs to keep out the night chill, had mumbled something in reply. His last words, indistinguishable. Raymond remembered seeing the bottles on the floor, the square darkness of the medicine and the tall fat brandy bottle, which he had bought that afternoon in response to his host's hints. They were sitting empty by the couch where the police had left them; he picked up the brandy and looked at it. *If I hadn't bought this Charlie would be alive today; you could say that I helped kill him.* But he could work up no excitement over this thought, could not tinge it with the power of fate. It was just something that happened and which could have had a million results. Perhaps because it happened to him, it seemed very ordinary.

The whole day, in fact, seemed ordinary. Where, he wondered, was the spectre of death he had heard about, the lurking menace of its presence that chills the hearts of men and makes dogs lie down and howl? Charlie might as well have gone away to visit a relative for all the effect it was having on him. He was puzzled and vaguely disappointed. It was the desire for the unusual that brought him to Australia in the first place, had made him squander his little inheritance on a trip through the most distant country he could think of. Finding a dead man on a couch was certainly unusual, but where was the reaction he had expected? Where was the awakening of some unsuspected character within his that the mystery of travel and adventure was supposed to bring? Raymond felt unchanged; he was still the same person who had been settling into the sediment of commuter life two weeks earlier, even though since then he had touched a dead man on the shoulder, shared a house with an illegal immigrant sailor, and successfully lied to the police. He knew that when he wrote back home about his time in Mt. Isa it would sound remarkable, but it drew no more reaction in him than had his visit to the Sydney Opera House.

He was mulling this over when the Swede suddenly appeared at the kitchen door. He did not have his bedroll with him and was slightly hesitant as he opened the screen, as if he feared Raymond would order him out. "Hello," he said carefully. Raymond feigned surprise. "Haven't the police found you yet?" The Swede started. "You told them about me?" "I couldn't help it—they had your description and a picture. They threatened to put me in jail if I didn't tell them." The Swede swore, a splash of angry Scandinavian consonants. "I will have to leave immediately. I cannot stay here." He was half out the door when Raymond began to laugh. For an instant he was very angry but then he laughed as well.

"You got me, with that one you got me!" he said over and over, sitting at the table and lighting a cigarette. "You got me very much. This morning I think you are making a joke when you are not, and now you make one and I do not suspect!" He offered the pack to Raymond, whom he knew did not smoke, and then put it back in his shirt.

"I couldn't resist—it was too good."

"The police did come?"

"Yes, but I didn't mention you. They didn't ask. You're okay, so far as I know."

The Swede had relaxed into a chair, slumping down as if felled by relief. "Good. Thank you. I am sorry to have left but I do not like to talk to the police for any matter. You understand?"

"Of course. Don't worry about it."

"Charlie, he is dead?"

"Yes. They think he drank that bottle of brandy I got him and a whole bottle of medicine and it killed him."

"A silly way to die. The end of a life should be more—more ---" he foundered for a word, shaping forms in the air with his hands.

"More dramatic?"

"Yes, like television. Explosions and things, that's how it should end." He shook his head. "But poor Charlie. He was a nice man."

"So what are you going to do now?"

"I am going south. I have met a man I think can give me a job. And you?"

"I'm taking the bus to Alice Springs this evening."

"More travelling. Good, good; it is good to see places." His cigarette finished, the Swede sat silent for a moment, drumming his fingers. Raymond suddenly knew what was coming. "Do you think perhaps you could let me have some money, maybe that ten dollars? We could pretend Charlie was not dead—that would be a good thing, Charlie to still be alive— and you could pay me the bet money."

Raymond stared down at his hands. "Boy, I don't know. I've got a long way to go—there's still a month on my visa— and I've got to make my money last. I don't really think I can spare..." There was nothing he could do if the Swede insisted and moved the matter into the arena of force, but he just shrugged and smiled. It didn't seem to matter that much to him. "I understand you. But I just thought I would ask." The subject closed, he looked idly around the room. "This house, it is different without our friend.'

"I was thinking that earlier. It's funny being here alone." Eager to leave the money issue behind, he gestured toward some of the signs. "I was looking through some of the stuff Charlie's painted over the years. Lots of it is real good." The Swede did not seem interested; signs to him were just signs. "What will they do with the house?"

"Mr. Bailey plans to rent it out again, I guess; I talked to him in the store. He's going to put together the funeral. If you're still around you can go to it." The Swede grinned at him. "Good idea. It is nice to have an arrest during a funeral— it makes things to be more lively." He ground out the cigarette. "No, I liked very much our friend Charlie but I do not think it would be a good idea to go to his funeral. He will not mind."

"He'd understand," Raymond agreed. "He didn't seem to care much about that sort of stuff."

"No, he did not. He just liked to meet people. It is not many who would take men from a bar, like you and me, and let them stay in his house for nothing, just because he likes people. Not many at all. We were lucky to meet him."

"Yes, we were lucky."

"Another few days and we would have missed him entirely!" The Swede threw himself back in his chair and laughed loudly at his own joke, so loudly that it drowned out the sound of knocking, and Raymond was not even sure he had heard it until the tentative little noise came again. He put up his hand. "Someone is at the front door. The Swede scrambled to his feet and looked out the window. "No police car," he murmured. He stood, half hiding in the kitchen as Raymond went to the front and carefully opened the door. He found a tiny woman, wrapped in a mélange of discarded clothing, standing at the bottom of the patchwork steps. She had been walking away but turned when the door opened and gaped up at Raymond.

"Yes?"

The woman stood and shuffled for a moment. "Is Mr. Pendergast here?" Her voice was as light as her knock, a wispy ghost of itself.

"You mean Charlie?" She nodded, a bobbing motion of the blue scarf around her pale face. "I'm sorry, but Charlie died last night in his sleep." She didn't move and he wasn't sure she had understood. She seemed half-witted. "Are you a friend of his?" She looked at the ground and whispered something. "What?" He bent down to hear better.

"He gives me his bottles."

"His bottles?"

"His medicine bottles." She showed a paper bag that

clinked when it moved. "He gives me them."

"Oh." Raymond was uncertain what to do. "But he isn't here anymore. He's dead."

Still looking down, the woman repeated, "He gives me his bottles," as if this answered all possible confusions.

"I see." He hesitated, then said, "Come inside. There is a bottle here you can have." The woman shuffled back up the steps and followed him down the hall, her cracked shoes raising dust from the floor. In the living room he gave her the medicine bottle. "Do you want this one, too? It had brandy in it."

She nodded and carefully put the bottle in her bag, which was half full of darkened glass and labels. Then she stood, motionless, while Raymond waited for her to do something, anything. Behind her the Swede stuck his head in the door and looked puzzled. Raymond looked back and shrugged and then the woman, with the air of repeating something imperfectly heard, said, "Charlie is dead?"

"Yes, I'm sorry. He died in his sleep. He wasn't in any pain or anything. Mr. Bailey will set up the funeral, if you want to go. Do you know Mr. Bailey?" The woman just stood silent, fingering her bag, which made little noises like a wind chime. Raymond could not guess her age; she could have been as old as Charlie, or not much older than himself. The Swede walked into the room, a smile on his face.

"He gives me his bottles," the woman said in a whisper, still staring at the floor. This struck the Swede as comic. "Not anymore!" he answered, and the woman jumped and stared at him in surprise. Her eyes were slightly crossed. "He always gives me them. He was nice to me." It was her first direct statement; the surprise seemed to have woken her up. She rummaged in her bag and pulled out a bottle like the one Raymond had just handed her. "He gave me this," she said, turning it slowly in her fingers. "In this room. He gave me this."

"And what did he want in return? A little—"the Swede said something in his native language and grinned at Raymond, but the woman paid him no attention. She put the bottle in the bag and looked at the ground. "I didn't know," she said.

"Know what"" Raymond asked.

"I didn't know he would die."

Raymond began, "None of us..." but she went on. "I didn't know it was the last time he would give me a bottle. He gives me his bottles, but that was the last time. The last time ever." She spoke slowly, as in a daze, and the Swede's grin broadened. But Raymond was not amused, for the words, with the curious power sometimes have to sink home where they have always glanced off before, to penetrate and carry ideas that have for years rested lightly on the surface, hit deep in his chest, and with them came the realization that one day he would do everything, no matter how trivial or important, for the last time. He had always known this, of course, but never *felt* it, that one day he would read a book for the last time, never to do it again; he would drive a car for the last time, and never drive again; he would eat his last meal, take his last shower, even make love for the last time, and when it was finished that would be the end of making love forever. The idea moved from his mind to his spirit, and when it did he learned what death is.

The knowledge filled his lungs and burned his eyes; he found it hard to draw a breath and for a moment he was blind and deaf. He did not hear the Swede asking the woman about her bottles, did not see her draw back in alarm, mumbling that it was her collection, that she had to go now, did not notice as she backed out of the room and down the hall, did not hear the front door carefully close and the laughing of the Swede. "Quite a bird, that one!" I wonder what she does with all those bottles; I bet she has a hundred at home. What do you think? Raymond? What is the matter?"

"Nothing. Nothing." He drew a deep breath and then another. "She was just kind of—just kind of pathetic."

"Pathetic?" The Swede was uncertain of the term. "She is ridiculous! But I think she does not know better so her life does not bother her. Many people, they are worse off, I think; do not worry yourself over it." He slapped Raymond on the shoulder. "It is getting late. The sun is almost setting." He motioned at the hallway, filled with floating dust particles given momentary substance by the nearly horizontal light. "Your bus leaves soon, I think."

"Yes. In an hour."

"Then why do we not leave here and get supper at the Miner's Bar? We can have a beer together—it will be our last." Raymond started. "What is wrong?"

"Nothing. That sounds fine. Let me get my bag."

The Swede followed him, puzzled. "You are being very strange suddenly. Do not worry, I will not ask you for money again." Raymond gathered up his things and they went out the back door, closing it behind them although there was no lock to secure. They walked slowly across the gravel lot, Raymond silent and the Swede uncertain. At the corner they turned and looked back at the house. The Swede, with sudden inspiration, said, "Maybe you are worried that I am going to pull a joke on you one last time to get back at you. Is that why you are so strange?"

"No, I am not thinking about jokes any more." In the yellow-red light of the evening the house seemed to glow. He could see the front steps where the old woman had gone down and the window of the room where Charlie had died, and he wondered how long it would be before his heart would not hang so heavy. "Let's go," he said, and in a moment they were gone.

The Human Cloud

By Bungalow Stokes

We found him in a corner of the Veterans Home,
wheelchair-bound, back rigid, jawbone jutting,
eyes like a shark's, black and empty,
looking through or past us.
His soul, what made him him, was
like an email that was sent but never received,
lost in the ether, either to reappear for a moment
or simply be gone — to the Great Perhaps perhaps?
His memories, the ones and zeroes of his self,
imprinted with a hardscrabble Depression life,
bathed in jar-borne corn from a still in the barn,
until he put down his hunting rifle and picked up an M-1.
His medals were misplaced, but he carried
once-smoking metal in his neck from the Bulge;
every winter his feet ached to the bone
jerking him back to the Ardennes in '44.
He was mute on such things for years,
or maybe we should have listened better.
His memories faded, from recent to deep past,
But wait! we are the human cloud.
He resides still, in high schools,
where his Polaroids of Nordhausen go up on the screen,
giving graphic reality of the Holocaust
to each new unknowing cohort.
Perhaps his soul has pushed on through the membrane
but his essence has gone viral.

BEYOND A SHADOW

By Asher Roth

The alert flashed on the cruiser's laptop, followed immediately by the radio dispatcher:

> Unit one thirty-three… four-fifteen in progress at Waterford Wal-Mart. Injury reported—paramedics en route.

Mike Fitzgerald had been an Oakland County sheriff's deputy for four years, and he loved every minute of it. There was something about the uncertainty—cruising through the suburban Michigan neighborhoods in his Crown Vic Interceptor, sometimes in tandem with senior partner Sgt. Tony Velasquez, never knowing what the day would bring. Maybe he was an adrenaline junkie—then again, so was Tony. So were most of the guys in his squad… hard to be a patrol cop and not enjoy living on the edge.

Oakland County bordered Detroit along 8 Mile Road. Unlike its bankrupt neighbor to the south, the county was one of the most prosperous in Michigan. With sixty townships and more than a million residents, it was home to the scions of the automotive industry. But even with its quiet cul-de-sacs and manicured lawns, Oakland was hardly a cakewalk: every emergency call carried its own risks.

There were the unpredictable encounters, like the six-foot-eight, three hundred pound intoxicated bar patron—a former defensive tackle for the Lions. It took both Mike and Tony to wrestle him to the ground, but not before the drunken ex-lineman threw a haymaker that broke the sergeant's nose, leaving it permanently crooked.

Then there was the close call in affluent Highland Hills, where Mike had to dive out of the path of an oncoming Escalade SUV driven by a texting sixteen-year-old who apparently didn't know that a cop in a reflective yellow vest standing in the middle of an intersection under a broken traffic light during a violent rainstorm with his hand raised and palm facing outward meant: STOP.

Every now and then, there were ones big enough to make the headlines—such as when Tony and Mike rescued a child who had fallen through the ice while skating on Crescent Lake. That bit of heroism earned them letters of commendation, and a short hospital stay for hypothermia.

And then there was the only time Mike had used his service automatic in the course of a crime.

It was a 415—disturbance call—at the Wal-Mart west of Waterford, in the middle of the county. He and Tony were the closest cruisers and the first to arrive on the scene. There was a sizable crowd standing around the front of the store, watching a pair of EMTs tend to a middle-aged woman wearing a Wal-Mart vest, sitting on the sidewalk. One of medics was bandaging her left arm.

A tall man also wearing an employee vest was kneeling next to the woman. He rose to meet the deputies at the entrance: his red, white, and blue Wal-Mart nametag displayed JERRY in large block letters. Printed on a yellow tag suspended underneath in smaller type was ASSISTANT MANAGER.

"Oakland County Police. What's the problem?"

"There's a guy with a knife in the Outdoors Department," Jerry replied, pointing into the store. He nodded toward the injured woman. "He attacked Anita—that's her over there with the paramedics—but she managed to get away. He's got some other people trapped inside."

The two deputies trotted through the expansive store, following the assistant manager. Tony was talking into his shoulder-mounted radio, keeping HQ apprised. Mike's right hand lightly rested on his holster as he ran. They slowed down as they approached the hanging sign displaying OUTDOORS, and Mike saw him before Jerry pointed: a large white male, brandishing a broad-bladed, gleaming hunting knife.

"He asked to see the knife... and then he started playing with it..." Jerry panted, slightly winded. "Anita was at the register... and she told him that she had to put the knife away... and he reached over the counter and cut her. He's got some people cornered near the wall."

Mike looked at his partner. "Should I flank him?"

"I'll do it. This one's yours," Tony said, turning and beginning to walk in a wide arc to the side of the knife-wielding man. Three people—a young man, a woman and a child—were cowering in a corner of the store. The little boy, maybe four years old, was whimpering. Mike guessed that they were a family. The store manager was standing a safe distance away, talking to the large man, who seemed to be ignoring him.

Mike unsnapped his Glock's holster and slowly walked over to the manager, whispering: "Oakland County Police. Tell me what's happening."

"A customer. He's got a knife. He's threatening that family... seems to know them. I'm trying to keep him calm, but I don't think he's listening to me."

"Do you know his name?"

The manager shook his head. "No, but I think the woman's been calling him Billy."

"Okay. You stay here. I'm going to approach him—you don't move, understand?"

The manager nodded.

Mike looked over at Tony, now positioned to the side of the man. The two deputies traded nods and Tony unholstered his gun. Mike started for his Glock, then thought better of it, reaching instead behind his back for the Taser. He cautiously advanced: the stun gun held rock-steady, aimed at the torso of the man standing over the family, glaring down at them.

"Billy? My name's Mike. I'm a police officer. I need you to put down the knife. Do you understand?"

"William," the man said, still staring at the family. "It's William."

Okay, asshole... William, Mike murmured to himself. "William, I need you to put the knife down, *now*. Do it *now*."

"No. She has to pay. They have to pay," William said.

Oh, Christ... domestic crap. Some sort of payback. Probably an affair... maybe his kid?

"We can work that out, but you need to put down that knife."

He had gradually advanced to within twenty-five feet of the man. No chance to tackle him—not with that knife in his hand. He was holding it like he knew how to use it. The Taser might reach, but twenty-five feet was dicey. He wondered whether he should inch closer, but the guy looked like he was on the verge of doing something, and Mike didn't want to force his hand. What if the Taser missed, or it couldn't stop him in time?

He slowly, silently reached behind his back, re-holstering the stun gun. He then grasped the grip of his Glock and lifted it out, aiming at the man's chest. "We can work this out, William," he repeated, "but you need to put that knife down, *now*."

"No," William said. "She needs to pay, *now*." He took a step toward the cringing family.

"*Stop! Drop the weapon!*" Mike barked.

The large man swiveled toward Mike. He raised his hand holding the knife.

Mike pulled the trigger. Twice. Three times.

The loud report sparked a chain reaction. Tony also discharged his weapon. In seconds, the two deputies fired seven rounds at the knife-wielding man.

Four of the bullets slammed into him. The other three missed their target.

One of these—forensics later determined it had been fired from Tony's gun—ricocheted off a display shelf.

Still intact, it traveled directly toward the family at a thousand feet per second.

It struck the left temple of the little boy, breaking into a dozen shards as it tore through his brain.

At first, there was complete silence. Then the large man began a low, monotonous groan, his life ebbing away. Mixed with this were the soft entreaties from the woman, saying her child's name over and over.

And then her wail began, like a siren approaching from the distance, becoming a scream that echoed through the store.

It echoed in Mike's head, still.

Witnesses later told police they thought the man might

have been raising his hand to show both officers that he was dropping the knife, not preparing to throw it.

* * *

Mike squinted, peering into the dimly-lit narrow bar, barely making out the hunched figure in the booth at the far end. Immediately after the incident, per protocol, both officers had been taken off patrol and assigned to different substations. As the inquiry progressed, they met after hours at *Boilermaker's*, in the lake region west of Pontiac. Mike had hoped these meetings would help them hammer things out… a kind of therapy. They were anything but.

"You look like crap," he said, sliding into the booth bench opposite Tony.

The older man barely nodded. Crap was an understatement. The amber light caught his etched face with its bent nose and grizzled cheeks as he slowly looked up from the Budweiser bottle clutched between his fleshy hands, scanning Mike's face. "So do you."

"Yeah, well, not as bad as you, I hope."

"Go look in a mirror," Tony said, taking a swig of his beer.

"How're they treating you at the station?"

"Same old shit—'Hey, Tony… How ya doin' Tony? How's the wife and kids?'"

At least he has a family, Mike thought. "They got you working anything?" he asked his sergeant.

"Nada. You?"

"Just paperwork. Hate it."

"Not even that for me." Tony's sallow, forlorn eyes reminded Mike of a bulldog. "They're putting me on disability."

Mike nodded. "Probably a good move. You really do look like hell."

"It's over," Tony said, draining his bottle. "They don't put you back out after that."

Mike was silent for a while, working through what he wanted to say. "I'm glad you gave me the lead. I wanted it."

"Doesn't matter... it was my call."

"Yeah, well, it was my call not to light him up. I took the first shot."

Tony gave a sickly smile and looked down, shaking his head.

"What can I get you, officers?" a waiter interrupted.

"Two 'makers," Mike replied. "Keep 'em coming."

"No," Tony raised his hand. "Bad with the meds. I'm done."

"Just one for me, then."

"On its way."

Mike waited until the server was out of earshot. "That *William* shithead... he knew what he was doing. The profile that IID ran on him... he was a hunter—a pro with knives. The kid was his... he was stalking them—cut the salesclerk just to bring us in. It's the only explanation. The asshole had a death wish."

Tony placed his head in his hands, rubbing his temples as Mike spoke. "Yeah, great. Tell me something new."

There wasn't anything new.

"It was mine," Tony finally broke the silence. "That's all that matters."

"You don't know that..." Mike protested. "*They* don't know that. Forensics isn't foolproof—it could've been mine."

"One hundred."

"What?"

"That's the hundredth time you've given me that shit. I've been keeping count. We both know it was mine."

"So what if it was? They said it was a one-in-a-million thing... an anomaly. You saw the report... that's what they called it—an anomaly."

"Fuck your anomaly!" Tony bellowed, rising from the booth, his uniform drawing stares from the other patrons. He pulled out his wallet, removed a twenty and pitched it onto the table. Then he pulled out another twenty, tossing it next to the first.

"Here, drink yourself to oblivion. I gotta get home."

The waiter returned with the boilermaker and Mike sat alone, nursing his drink, thinking through the scene that unfolded in slow motion in his head, like an NFL replay stuck in a perpetual loop—

That asshole was going to throw it... something about the twist of his wrist, the jerk of his arm, the arch of his body... the others couldn't see it. He had to be throwing it.

What if it really was my bullet that hit the kid? Maybe forensics was wrong. Angles can be deceptive.

The inquiry lasted two months, Internal Affairs concluding that the shooting was a justifiable use of deadly force during an authorized police action. The sheriff's department issued a mild reprimand to Tony for delegating the lead to a junior officer, and it questioned Mike's decision to forgo the Taser, but no fault was found in the actions of either deputy, and no disciplinary measures were taken.

After the report was published, Mike was given a desk working cold cases—a one-year probationary period before he was reassigned—and Tony retired from the force on disability.

The sergeant was still receiving counseling for the little boy's death when he drove along Lake Shore Drive on a late afternoon in early autumn, parking in a small wooded area bordering Lake St. Clair.

His gait stiff but resolute, the sergeant followed a narrow trail to a gazebo overlooking the lake. The setting sun was turning the willow oaks a lush golden hue, a slight breeze making the water shimmer and glint in a thousand diamonds. Geese crossing the lake caught the waning sun's warm rays— their distant, plaintive calls a soft accent to the leaves rustling overhead and waves lapping against the shore. Taking out his cell phone, he dialed 911.

Nine-one-one. What is your emergency?

"Eleven-ninety-nine. Officer down, Lake Shore and Fairway Circle. Eleven forty-one—request backup and EMT, STAT."

Without hanging up, Tony set the phone on the gazebo's bench, calmly waiting several minutes until he could hear the soft wail of sirens approaching in the distance. Tears streaming down his cheeks, he lightly touched the rosary beads in his pocket, quietly reciting the *Ave Maria*. He then placed the barrel of a Smith and Wesson .38 Special into his mouth and pulled the trigger.

A note found on his body, addressed to the couple and penned in a drugged scrawl, said simply:

"Please, please forgive me."

*   *   *

Maybe cold cases just weren't his thing. There was a small, tight-knit group of detectives in the Sheriff's Office who seemed to enjoy digging through old files, trying to uncover clues that might have been missed during prior investigations. It was a bit like searching for artifacts on an archeological dig, or piecing together an elaborate jigsaw puzzle. But shoveling dirt and matching odd-shaped cutouts weren't two of Mike's favorite activities. True, finding something that might help to clear up mysteries from the past had its rewards: thankful relatives; praise from the DA's office; maybe even a blurb in the paper. But months could go by without any discoveries, retreading well-worn paths long ago abandoned. Plus, it was a bit overwhelming—entering a room filled with cardboard boxes piled on a table brimming with case-study folders, court documents, miscellaneous newspaper clippings, autopsy reports, and tagged evidence bags.

It required lots of reading. That also wasn't his thing. His eyes would become crossed after just a few pages of court transcripts and forensic reports. He'd become a coffeeholic—not from lack of sleep, but needing the caffeine to help him stay focused on the paperwork. Well… maybe a lack of sleep, too. He hadn't slept well since the Wal-Mart shooting. Tony's suicide had made it worse.

"You need any help?"

Mike looked up from the 1998 child abduction file. Detective Bob Frankel was peering over his shoulder. Frankel had been Mike's mentor during the past nine months, ever since he was pulled off patrol and given a desk. He had helped Mike through Tony's death as well.

"You've been staring at that sheet for several minutes, Mikey. Zoned out?"

Mike put down the paper and rubbed his eyes. "Yeah, guess so." He picked the report back up. "Hard that they're all majors."

"Statute of limitations. The hangers-on are mostly rapes, kidnappings, homicides."

Mike nodded. "Yeah… figures. Man, tons of missing child reports—never realized how many. Not something I ran into much on the beat."

"That's because they're the hardest to crack. And the older they get, the colder."

"Must be living hell for their parents. Years looking, turning into decades… not even children any more—if they're still alive. They're like ghosts, in a way… I feel like they're hovering over the boxes, begging me to find them."

For the thousandth time, images of the little boy splayed prone in a pool of blood on the store's hard linoleum flashed through his mind. *At least there wasn't any waiting—zero uncertainty.* He shook his head. *What the fuck difference did that make? Her child, brutally torn from her in an instant…*

Bob slapped his back. "You need a break, my friend."

"Thanks, I'm okay," Mike insisted. "Just need to focus."

Better hold it together if I'm ever getting out of this muck and back on patrol. Three more months till final review.

Rape and homicide cases offered more material to trowel through, though rarely more hope. Witnesses were long gone, and when one or two could be located, their memories of events were clouded by time. The best hope for these cases rested in the collected evidence, and the best evidence was hair, blood and semen.

DNA analysis was reaching full maturity, with microscopic skin particles embedded in sweat stains yielding results. Detailed profiles now pinpointed an individual without any of the "probability" uncertainties that had confounded investigators and exasperated judges in the technology's infancy. Genetic fingerprinting had become so reliable, it was being treated as gospel by the courts: prisoners incarcerated decades ago based on circumstantial evidence were now exonerated and freed by a swatch of semen-soaked cloth, or a scraping from a victim's fingernails—all meticulously collected and documented by the original detectives assigned to the case, and preserved in evidence bags over the intervening years.

While the unjustly convicted were being proven innocent, there was another side to the coin: proof of guilt. With DNA analysis virtually infallible, those who had escaped punishment for so long could now be brought to justice. Their day of reckoning had finally arrived.

DNA profiling was the crucial cog, but what made the system click was the network: the compilation and sharing of DNA records from millions of people, all stored on computers and fed into a database that could be accessed by any agency, from the FBI down to local jurisdictions. This, combined with the immense processing power of computers, made DNA matching almost instantaneous. It was a great time to be a cop with a sample of a perp's DNA, and a very bad time to be a killer on the lam with your DNA stored in the system.

"Next one, Mikey," Frankel announced the following Monday, holding out a dog-eared manila folder. "Not much to go on with this one, I'm afraid. Dates back to nineteen eighty-five. Twenty-nine years... even before my time, believe it or not."

"That *is* hard to believe," Mike chuckled, taking the folder. "What is it?"

"Homicide. Young woman… a girl, really. Pretty brutal. Possible rape attempt. I got it on the last review, back in '04. Didn't get any further than the first go-around. Maybe you'll have better luck."

"Yeah, right," Mike said. "Ten more years really helps these things."

"Everything's in one box in the evidence room. Have fun."

Mike paged through the worn folder: brutal murder of a teenager named Lucreisha Parker near the city line. As Frankel had mentioned, possibly attempted rape—more likely a john or some PCP-drenched junkie taking their anger out on her. According to the autopsy report, the killer was a big brute, left-handed, judging from the location and force of the blows. Lucreisha had fought back, grabbing the shirt of her assailant and tearing off a patch that was still gripped in her hand when the deputies found her. She was splayed between two dump-sters in an alleyway next to an abandoned package store and a pawn shop in Royal Oak, just north of 8 Mile Road. Lucreisha was only sixteen when she was murdered: a part-time prosti-tute and drug addict with no fixed address, living off the street. She might have known her assailant—she might not. Possibly a chance encounter, or a relationship gone sour… or a pimp or dealer who didn't get their money. Two blocks farther south and it would have been Detroit's problem, not theirs.

In the evidence room, he studied the transparent evidence bag holding the torn piece of cloth. It was yellowed with age, but still spattered with blood. A portion of a stenciled college logo could be seen: forensics had identified it as Jessup Com-munity College, not far from where she was murdered. The logo must have been located on the portion of the t-shirt where a pocket usually goes: apparently, she had grasped the assailant's shirt with her right hand, ripping the material in her desperate fight for life. Mike always had a strange feeling when looking at evidence like this: a testament of a moment in time, primitively brutal—a silent, unerring record of a struggle to the death. It turned out that the blood on the shirt wasn't hers: the blood type didn't match.

During Frankel's review ten years earlier, they had run a full DNA profile, but it failed to find a match among the few suspects who had provided samples. As often happened with victims who didn't have family to continually pressure the Sheriff's office, the case re-entered the purgatory of unsolved, gathering dust until the rotation cycle brought it back to the top of the pile.

A great deal had changed in the intervening years: not only was DNA profiling far more precise, but there was also the database. Instead of a handful of suspects, now there were millions.

He called the crime lab. The station's young forensic technician answered the phone.

"Hey, Jackie, can you run an STR on some blood from a cold case I'm working?"

"For you, Mike, anything. What's the incident?"

"Murder. Some kid on the street. Young hooker."

"How old?"

"Sixteen, I think."

"No," she laughed. "I mean, when did it happen?"

"Oh… nineteen eighty-five."

"How big a sample are we talking about?"

"Plenty big. Several good-sized drops and one big splotch on a shirt fragment."

"Shouldn't be a problem. It's a slow day—bring it on

down."

Mike signed for the evidence bag with the duty clerk and took the elevator down to the lab. He found Jackie dressed in her lab coat seated on a high stool at one of the stainless steel tables, completing some paperwork: a pair of sleek, long legs extended from a teasingly short mid-thigh pencil skirt.

"You got it there?" she asked.

Mike nodded. "This is it. About all the evidence left from this one."

"No scrapings, hair, anything to match it against?"

"Nope. Not that I could find in the box. Nada."

She held the bag up to the light. "Well, it's certainly a big enough sample. I'm guessing none of this is the victim's?"

"Nope. Blood type was different."

She placed the bag on the table next to her. "Nice of the perp to bleed all over his shirt for us. Sign here. I should have this back for you by next week."

Mike let out a low whistle. "Man, it gets faster and faster!"

Jackie glanced around the lab, then gave him a wry smile, whispering: "Almost as fast as you."

Mike also looked around to see whether anyone had entered the lab, then leaned over and gave her a kiss on the cheek. "It's already faster than that!"

"In your dreams," she said, wistfully. "Or rather, in *my* dreams."

"Oh?" Mike asked, slightly hurt. "I can slow it down. I'm only here to please you."

She smirked. "Is that so? I'm going to carve that into my headboard, so you remember it next time... if there *is* a next time."

"Oh, there'll be a next time. How about Friday... pick you

up at seven, dinner at The Village Green, then either dancing at Twenty-Twenty, or drinks at Polo House—your call."

"Mmm... you do know my soft spots! Okay, you have yourself a deal... but remember what you said. I'm going to Home Depot for a hammer and chisel after work tonight."

"It's already chiseled up here," Mike said, pointing to his head as he walked out of the lab.

Jackie was waiting for him at his desk Friday morning, cradling a flash drive between her thumb and forefinger. "The sample was cleaner than I expected. They only needed two runs to verify the STR sequences."

"You really are the best!" Mike said, taking the drive from her.

"Oh, I know that," she smiled. "I have that stenciled in my bedroom, too."

"You do? I never noticed it."

She scanned the almost-empty open office. "It's on the ceiling," she whispered. "You never look up there."

"Well," Mike winked, whispering back, "we'll have to fix that. Next time, you drive."

Jackie looked around once more, her cheeks reddening. "Okay, back to business, Casanova. I have other things on that drive, so download the data and hand it back."

"You could have just uploaded this to the server, you know."

"Yes, I suppose I could have, but then I wouldn't be able to help you search."

Mike raised his eyebrows. "Oh? We're partnering on this?"

"Like I told you, it's been slow in the lab. I don't mind lending a hand." She shot him a glance. "That is, if you want it."

"I'd love it! It'll go twice as fast."

"Oh no," she laughed. "I am *not* getting into that with you again!"

She snatched the flash drive back from him, sat down at his desk and plugged it into the USB port on his laptop.

Working the keyboard, she linked into the CODIS system on the National DNA Database. Almost immediately, the laptop received a match—what was known in the field as a cold hit:

Name: William Lamont Brawley
Birthdate: 06-15-1963
Age: 51
Race: African American
LKA: 4217 Park Ridge Road, Mason, MI 48854

Mike stared at the screen in disbelief.

Whoa.

Mason was only fifty miles west of Oakland County.

1963... that made him twenty-two in 1985, when the murder occurred.

The first name twinged a raw nerve. Mike's thoughts flashed back to the Wal-Mart shooting.

William... it's William.

Okay, asshole... William.

The DNA marker matchup was perfect. Probability of error was 1:56,278,455,617,924

He counted the comma sets—one in fifty-six *trillion*. As good as it gets.

"Are you believing this?" He looked over at Jackie. She

was also staring at the screen, wide-eyed.

"I've never seen it carried to the thirteenth power," she said.

"So, I'm guessing this is our guy?"

"Based on that number alone, it's unquestionable."

Jackie pushed the chair away from the desk and stood, as Mike traded places with her.

"Time to call up *William's* rap sheet," he said.

He ran a statewide check on Brawley. What he found made his fingers tingle:

```
Brawley, William L.
Arrest record:
1978: Simple assault. Convicted as minor.
Probation.
1978: Aggravated assault. Convicted as minor.
Probation with community service.
1979: Motor vehicle theft. Convicted as mi-
nor. Served 4 months: WCYCI.
1980: Aggravated assault. Convicted as minor.
Served 6 months: WCYCI.
1982: Felonious drug possession: Sched II
controlled substance. Served 2 years: SPSM,
MDOC.
2010: DUI Misdemeanor. Pleaded guilty. Proba-
tion with community service.
```

WCYCI was the Wayne County Youth Correctional Institute. Known as the Wayne County Reform School back then, it was the depository for most of Detroit's inner-city kids who got themselves into trouble. Not terrible by reform schools standards, but no great shakes, either. Considering the conditions at home for many of these kids, it probably seemed like a resort.

SPSM, on the other hand, was nobody's idea of a resort. The State Prison of Southern Michigan was a massive, brick-walled prison, built back in the nineteen-thirties. Not a pleasant place to do time. The complex was closed in 2007, soon after a mentally ill prisoner died there, tied naked for days to a concrete slab and left to soak in his own urine.

Mike sighed heavily. *That place could make a killer out of anyone.*

It was from Brawley's arrest in 2010 on the DUI that his DNA had entered the database. Without that, there was no sampling, and no match.

Thanks for driving drunk, William.

"That's funny," Jackie mused, peering at the screen over Mike's shoulder.

"What's funny?"

"Well, his DNA was collected from the DUI, so it really isn't supposed to be in CODIS. That's only supposed to be used for felony convictions. There's this whole controversy about how CODIS has a 'shadow' DNA database, listing people who shouldn't be in there. I suppose that, technically, it applies to our Mr. Brawley, here."

"Well, shadow or not, it's there."

"True enough," Jackie said, reaching over to the side of the laptop and unplugging the flash drive. "I have to get back to the lab. Looks to me like we've got our man."

"You've got that right," Mike smiled. "Nice when these cold ones get a break—especially for murder. Doesn't happen too often."

"We struck gold this time, babe," Jackie said, pinching his cheek. "And it's Friday. I've chosen Twenty-Twenty—I want to drink *and* dance!"

"You got it," Mike said, winking at her. "Fast dance, slow dance, and every speed in between."

"Oooh…" she cooed. "That one's definitely going on my headboard… and my ceiling, too!"

Over the course of the day, Mike ran a complete check on Brawley, and a picture of the man's life began to coalesce:

He was born in one of Detroit's poorest black neighborhoods, the youngest of six children. His father was a janitor at a public school; his mother did piecemeal embroidery while watching the children and keeping house—if you could call it a house: it was a tenement apartment in the projects. His dad skipped out soon after William was born, and the family went on welfare. None of the children finished high school… except for William, who went back to school after doing his stints at the youth correctional institute.

Must've found religion in the lockup, Mike mused.

Brawley received his HSED while serving time at Southern Michigan, and went on to enroll in a two-year college not long after his release in 1984, according to his parole report.

Jessup Community College.

Goddamn, Mike chuckled. *This one's solving itself.*

There were no convictions after 1982, other than the DUI.

Kept his nose clean after Lucreisha's death—or figured out how to stay below the radar. I would, too, with Murder One over my head.

Brawley had held a series of odd jobs during college, mostly through parole services and MDRC-sponsored workfare programs. After receiving his associate degree in 1988, he landed a position in the mailroom at a GM parts supplier, and then slowly worked his way up the ladder—Detroit was experiencing a short-lived revitalization back then, with the recently constructed Renaissance Center. By the mid-90's, Brawley was assistant manager in the mailroom. Over the next few years, he transferred to another auto supplier when the first went belly-up, slowly migrating west of the city. He was married by that point, with a family.

A family man. Thriving, watching ball games, playing with his kids, enjoying life, while Lucreisha rotted away in the ground. Now it was time, William—way past time, to pay the piper.

He took a break and called Jackie, filling her in on the details he'd discovered.

"This is absolutely amazing!" she exclaimed. "We hear about this all the time down in the lab—detectives stop by to thank us, and of course we have to testify in court at times, but I've never gotten to watch it all fall into place, especially with such an old case!"

"Well, this one's the exception. They're never this cut-and-dry."

"Can you imagine? He didn't even move out of the area—just went on with his life, like it never happened. What kind of person does that?"

"We're about to find out," Mike said. "I'm filing for an arrest warrant."

Two Michigan state troopers picked him up at his house: a modest rancher in Mason on a quiet residential street. They put him in cuffs, telling his wife that they were taking him to Oakland County for questioning.

"Questioning for what?" she asked one of the troopers.

"Murder investigation, ma'am."

"Murder? Whose murder?"

"I'm sorry ma'am. I can't give you any details."

She turned to her husband. "What's this about, William?"

"No idea. I don't know anythin' about no murder."

They placed a hand over his bald head, guiding him as he squeezed his large frame into the back of the squad car for the hour drive east, his family watching from the front door of the rancher.

In the sparse room, illuminated by a single large fluorescent ceiling fixture over the laminated table, Mike finished reciting the Miranda litany.

"Do you understand these rights as they have been read to you?"

The large black man nodded.

"You need to say it out loud, for the microphone."

"Yeah, I understan' all that crap."

"Do you want an attorney present for this?"

Brawley shook his head.

Mike was taken aback—in his five years on the force, only a handful of perps had waived an attorney. No one in their right mind agreed to direct questioning, especially on a major felony charge. He looked back at mirror-paneled wall behind him and shrugged, then turned back to Brawley. "Again, you need to say it out loud."

"No, no attorney. I got nothin' to hide. Ain't never killed nobody. I been clean ever since State—well, 'cept for that drunk drivin' thing. This about that?"

Mike shook his head. "No, no it isn't about that." He slid a small photo encased in plastic over to Brawley: an old black and white high school class photo, taken before she had dropped out of school and become a prostitute. It was the only photo they had of her alive. "Tell me about her."

Brawley rubbed his wrists where the cuffs had chafed him during the hour-long drive to Oakland County. He looked down at the picture. "Who is she?"

"You know who she is. Nineteen eighty-five. Royal Oak. Sweet Sixteen."

Brawley looked at him blankly. "Nineteen eighty-five? You crazy, man? That's like, what? Thirty years ago?"

"Twenty-nine," Mike said. "Twenty-nine years, *William*."

Brawley squinted at the mirrored wall, trying to make out who was on the other side. "Don't know who she is. Never seen her before."

"Look at the picture again. Take a closer look."

Brawley glanced back down at the passport-sized photo. "No idea."

"Maybe this will help," Mike said. He reached into the case folder and pulled out several more photos, spreading them in front of Brawley.

They were also of Lucreisha, taken at the murder scene and at the morgue. Brutally beaten, her face misshapen by a broken jaw. A dark indigo contusion covered a large sunken area, caused by a shattering blow to her right cheek.

Brawley glimpsed down at them, then quickly looked away.

Mike studied him. "You're a big guy, *William*—you're left-handed, aren't you?"

Brawley nodded. "So?"

"What was her name?"

"Huh?"

"Her name—what was her name?"

Brawley shook his head. "How the hell should I know? I told you I never seen her before!"

"Uh-huh. Right. We have your shirt, *William*... the shirt you wore when you did this. It has your blood on it." Mike leaned over the table so that his face was just inches away from Brawley's. "*Your* blood!"

"What the hell you talkin' 'bout, man? What shirt?"

Mike reached into the evidence bag and lifted out the shirt swatch, also sealed in plastic. He slid it across the table to Brawley.

"Look familiar?"

The large black man stared down at the yellowed fragment. He shook his head.

"It's your shirt, *William*. That's your blood all over it."

"Not my shirt. Not my blood."

"It's your blood, all right. Do you know what DNA profiling is?"

"I know what DNA is."

"Well, profiling is when a lab analyzes DNA—like your blood, here—and they determine what the chances are that it could be someone else's blood. Do you know what the chances are that this is somebody else's blood, other than yours?"

Brawley shook his head.

"Zero," Mike said. "Absolute zero. Can you make out the logo on there?"

Brawley looked at the fragment and again shook his head.

"What college did you go to, *William*?"

"Jessup," Brawly answered. "Why you keep stressin' my name like that?"

"Because I like your name, *William*," Mike sneered. He pointed at the piece of shirt. "That just happens to be Jessup Community College's logo."

"So? Lots of people went to Jessup."

"Yeah, maybe so," Mike said, still sneering, "but they didn't go around wearing t-shirts covered with your blood."

"Look, man, I don't know nothin' about this," Brawley said, almost pleading. "You said this was twenty-nine years ago, man. How the hell could I remember somethin' from that long ago?"

"You don't remember wearing this shirt, this sixteen-year-old girl tearing it, screaming, begging you to stop? You don't remember any of that?" Mike leaned across the table again. *"She was sixteen, William, only sixteen years old!"*

He snatched the fragment off the table and placed it back in the evidence bag, then held the bag aloft. "Yesterday or twenty-nine years, you don't forget killing someone, *William*. I know that you remember. Your shirt brought us to you, and it's going to make you pay."

"I think I want that attorney now," Brawley mumbled. "I think I made a big mistake sayin' no."

The trial lasted two and a half weeks, the twelve jurors deliberating only three hours to arrive at their verdict: murder in the second degree. Brawley's defense team had tried to argue that posting his DNA in the CODIS database violated his right to privacy, because it was collected in the course of a misdemeanor investigation and conviction, and not from a felony as required under the statute. Their objection was overruled by the judge, who cited Brawley's prior felony convictions as sufficient justification to include his DNA in the database.

The prosecution asked for thirty years, but the judge noted Brawley's nearly stellar conduct during the past three decades, including his holding a responsible job and raising a family. Even so, she declared, justice must be paid. He was sentenced to fifteen years at the G. Robert Cotton Correctional Facility in Jackson, Michigan, chosen for its proximity to his family in Mason. His first eligibility for parole would be in eight years, in the spring of 2022.

They were waiting for Mike when he arrived back at the station. Standing around his desk, they broke into applause as he entered the open office.

"Way to go, Mike," Detective Frankel said, handing him a cigar.

"Fifteen years, out in eight with good behavior," Captain Tom Landau added, giving Mike a good-natured slap on the back. "Not too shoddy, considering the time that's passed."

"Justice served this time, Mike," one of the lieutenants agreed. "Way to go."

Justice. Eight years for savagely beating a young girl to death. Eight lousy years for taking another person's life.

Still, he felt a sense of accomplishment. A debt, of sorts, had been paid—to Lucreisha and to society. Twenty-nine years late, but still it got paid.

He rolled the cellophane-wrapped cigar between his fingers. This one might get him promoted to detective.

Detective Fitzgerald. It had a nice ring to it.

Maybe being stuck at a desk digging through cold cases wasn't so bad after all.

*   *   *

It was getting late in the day, the sun beginning to draw long shadows on the pavement surrounding the basketball courts off Cherrylawn Avenue in the Palmer Park section of Detroit. The oppressive August heat lingered, the high humidity making sweat stick to the body like a second skin. The entire summer of 1985 had been unbearably hot.

On his way home from the community college two blocks from the city line, having just finished his finals, the young man stopped to watch the pickup game from behind the chain-link fence—three on three, Converses squeaking on the blacktop with each swivel and leap, mixing with the intermittent thump-thumps of the dribbled ball and the panting groans of the players—pointing, feinting a pass, then breaking for a layup.

"Dat's game, niggas—yo' cain't play shit!"

"Damn, Tyrone—I be wide open, man!"

"Yo' bitch's tang be wide open!"

"Shit—don't be hackin' flack w'dat smack, mofo!"

"You was hackin' me all game, DeShawn. Half-steppin', such…"

"Yo' cain't shoot shit, Bobby! Jez 'cause yo' chokin' on th' bunnies, don' be baggin' on me!"

The six sauntered off the court, picking up the t-shirts they had long-ago removed, and wiping their faces and shoulders.

"Ball up—we gonna cock yo' ass this time!"

"Man, I gotta sit this one out!" Mohammad moaned.

"Yeah, yo' take a break, ol' man. Yo' ain't doin' shit anyway!"

They looked around for a third to make the next game and spied him watching them from outside the fence. They were sizing him up, since he wasn't from their hood.

"Hey, cuz, how's it hangin'?" called out the one named DeShawn.

The young man gave DeShawn a quizzical look and pointed to himself. "Me?"

"Yeah, what's goin' down?"

"Nuthin'… just comin' thru."

DeShawn tucked the ball under his arm and walked over to the fence. "Yo' a big dude. Wanna slam a few?"

The young man hesitated for a moment. He was no stranger to street ball, having played countless half-court pickup games as a teen, and almost daily during his stint in the pen. Plus, with the summer semester finally over, it was time to unwind.

He nodded. "Uh, sure, yeah."

DeShawn pointed at his shirt. "What dat thang on there?"

The young man looked down to where the other man was pointing. "What? You mean this here symbol? It's Jessup Community College, man."

"Oh, yo' college boy?"

He nodded. "Yeah, I go there."

DeShawn eyed him suspiciously. "Yo' a fuckin' Oreo, man?"

"Nah… just like you, man."

"What's yo' name, blood?"

"Willy."

"Well, c'mon college boy, ball up!"

The young man walked around the fence and entered the court, electing to keep his t-shirt on. As with most pickup games in this part of the city, it was rough play, with almost every move involving some hard physical contact. It was clear that the other players knew each other—not only by their belligerent banter, but their playing style as well. The game was to eleven points, with layups counting one point and everything outside the arc, two. Willy's team fared poorly in the early going, quickly falling behind six-to-two.

"C'mon, college boy!" badgered DeShawn, who was playing on the other team. "Yo' a big-ass mofo—big as me! Shoot lefty like me, too! Put yo' 'nads in it!"

So Willy kicked it up a notch, squaring off with DeShawn and trading move for move. But switching to more aggressive play had the unfortunate consequence of making him drop his defenses, and he didn't see DeShawn's high elbow heading for his face until too late.

It landed squarely on his nose. Almost immediately, blood started pouring out, the droplets splattering his t-shirt. He quickly lifted off his shirt and balled it up into a wad, pressing it tightly against his nostrils to stanch the flow.

"Aw, you done clock his grill, man!" Tyrone exclaimed.

"Tain't his grill. Be his beak." DeShawn laughed.

The game momentarily stopped as Willy walked over to the bench and sat with his head pointed skyward. He was prone to bloody noses. It was so common that he'd lost count long ago of the times this had happened—particularly in prison—and he knew that the bleeding would stop as quickly as it had started. After a minute, with the other players teasing him about the mishap, he pulled the bloodied shirt away and tentatively checked his injury. Sure enough, the bleeding had ceased, and after sitting for another minute he was able to resume play. His team still lost the game, badly. After two more losses, he decided to call it quits and left, grabbing his bunched-up shirt from the bench.

It wasn't until he had reached his bus stop several blocks away and shaken out the shirt to put it on, that he realized he'd accidentally picked up someone else's t-shirt.

Back on the basketball court, having gotten his second wind, Mohammad rejoined his teammates and they played three more games before breaking off. Exiting the court, each of them grabbed their t-shirts off the bench, except DeShawn.

"Where my fuckin' threads?" he demanded.

"There," said Mohammad, pointing at the remaining top.

"Dat ain't mine," DeShawn said, picking it up and shaking it open. "Damn! Dis dat nigga's bloody tee!"

"He musta got yours," Bobby said. Everyone but DeShawn broke out in laughter.

"Yeah, so, dat's okay," DeShawn replied, starting to grin. "Dis one better anyway. Look—it got dat college thang on't. I be goin' t' college!"

And he put the shirt on, the blood on the front still glistening.

"Oh, dat's jus' fuckin' gross, man!" Tyrone said. "You be gettin' his blood on you!"

"Yeah, so what?" DeShawn answered, still grinning. "It's like my prize o' war! Dis gonna be my lucky tee!"

❧

Startime

By Bungalow Stokes

Calm. Ultimate calm.

Four o'clock in the morning. The ensign was sitting at the bow of the aircraft carrier, the ship cutting through the South China Sea almost noiselessly, in spite of its seventy thousand tons, plowing a thirty-five-foot deep furrow in the ocean. There were no lights—not from the ship; not from other ships; and not from some distant shoreline. Never had the ensign seen so many stars, horizon to horizon. There was no moon this night, and the dark sky melded into the darker sea.

As the ship's bow wake disturbed the fluorescence of the sea, it looked as though thousands of submerged flash bulbs were popping all around. The breeze was only that created by the moving ship—about sixteen refreshing knots.

The ensign remembered this same hour, four months ago, when he first went to the charthouse to begin making a name for himself. He had made his way inside the superstructure, over the knee-knockers, though the watertight mechanical doors, up the too-steep ladders to the chartroom. Here he hailed the Master Chief.

"Good morning, Master Chief. I'm ready."

The Master Chief was a big man, nearing three hundred pounds, in his mid-thirties and well-weathered. He was an intimidating man. From his crew-cut form came a booming voice.

"You *think* you're ready."

It was just before dawn. The ensign had been reviewing his textbook on how to shoot stars. The Master Chief was the teacher, albeit a reluctant one. For him, this was a chore. These young naval officers would come to him for a few days, just long enough to get their qualification book signed off. They had to demonstrate that they knew something about the ways of finding out where in the ocean they were. They would talk about the electronic means, whereby the ship's location could be pinpointed from satellite signals. But even in this day and age there needed to be someone onboard who knew celestial navigation, the ancient art of using the stars to find your way. At this the Master Chief was unsurpassed. And it was at this the ensign was determined to make a statement.

He had nearly failed his college navigation course, and was almost kicked out of the officer training program. Now he was out to prove he belonged. He wasn't merely going to qualify; he was going stun the quartermaster world.

When still in college, the only thing the ensign-to-be really mastered was how to get by. He would write papers the night before they were due. He would pull all-nighters before the final exams. Before one final exam he got drunk, and turned his class grade from an A to a D in one sitting. The goal back then was clear: do what had to be done, then play basketball, or pick up a guitar, or party. Nietzsche, no... Booker T and the MGs, yes!

He and his fellow partiers, the self-named Dawn Patrol, lived by a motto: "If the minimum wasn't good enough, it wouldn't be the minimum." In the task of navigating a ship, however, he knew there was no "just getting by." You either knew where you were or you were lost in the vast ocean.

The art of celestial navigation involved an instrument called a sextant: a protractor-like precision device with a split-view optical piece. The sailor would select one of several stars he would find, or "shoot," in one lens and then line it up with the horizon in the other. When he checked the reading on the protractor, he knew the angle from the horizon to the star. This bit of information was the key. Armed with the readings for several stars, the navigator would run some calculations and then plot a line for each star on a map of the ocean, called a chart. The intersection of those lines on the chart was the ship's whereabouts. The ability to line up the images in the eyepiece was what would make or break the result.

With the smoothness of watch gears the Master Chief located the position of each designated star.

"Mark!" he sang out as he swung the sextant, pivoting it at the top so that the arc he swung just touched the image of the horizon. The exact time and the sextant reading were carefully noted by the quartermaster as the Master Chief moved through his paces.

When it was the ensign's turn, he looked hopeless, even spasmodic. He moved his head up and down, searching for the correct star through the instrument's eyepiece. His head snapped this way and that, like a chicken in a barnyard. He could not find any star, much less the correct ones, nor could he relate it to the horizon. The Master Chief and the quartermaster ducked into the chartroom before they embarrassed the young man by laughing out loud. However, the scene of an officer in the United States Navy standing outside in the dark throwing his head up and down like a one-armed oil rig was too much.

Upon moving to the chartroom to use the data, the men

ran calculations that translated the sextant information into lines on the chart. The Master Chief's lines all met in one point. Perfect. *This* was where the ship was, precisely. On the other hand, the ensign's lines formed a massive triangle. Theoretically at least, the center of this triangle was the ship's location. Truly the ensign had erred; they were most definitely not sailing through Nevada. Indeed, left to his own skills, the ensign did not know where the hell he was.

But that was then.

*

*

*

*

*

*

*

*

The ensign pushed REWIND in his mind: months earlier, in a rented house in San Leandro, California.

Frenzy. Absolute frenzy. The volume of the music was making the walls hum. The outstretched arms of the dancing throng reached into the air, and sometimes, when the dancers were on the counters, the couches, and the fireplace mantle, they reached to the ceiling. The frenzy was fueled primarily by a recipe that the owners of the house called Jet Fuel: a sneaky concoction of grain alcohol and fruit, such as lemons picked off the trees right outside the back door. Sprite may have been an ingredient, though the proportions were at best inexact.

It was a month before the ship was scheduled to leave to the Far East. They would soon enough be "out there," participants in the Cold War, staring into the godless face of international communism. For now, the standing orders stated, Party.

The ensign and his housemates, Coconut and The Padre, opened up their rented San Leandro house to their friends and colleagues from the ship, and any and all of their friends. Coconut was the first person the ensign met in California; they had arrived at the aircraft carrier for duty the same day. Coconut, a New Yorker, with his shaved head (thus the nickname) and baby face, was a prime mark for single women. He was also a virgin, leaving many a date frustrated, as well as his friends who were in disbelief at his willpower. He claimed it was because he wanted to be a priest if the Navy thing didn't work out.

Lieutenant Bill Danwell, aka The Padre (so-called because of his calm, seemingly reverent, demeanor), joined in on the house rental because he needed a place off the ship to get high. Mostly the rituals of the Friar of the Fleet occurred in his room or on the back patio. On party nights, though, he ministered to the assembled flock.

On any such party night, perhaps eighty people would come and go throughout the evening, until the occasion fizzled in the wee hours.

At several previous events, the police had shown up. Nobody ever knew who called them, although anyone would agree it was necessary. It's just that the neighbors liked the guys who lived there. They were looked upon as good neighbors who were serving their country. So what if they got loud every now and then? Even the police who came by liked them.

Neighbors sneaking a peak out their darkened windows would often see the officers imploring the ensign in a good-natured way to put a lid on the noise. It was always the ensign who spoke with the police. The Padre would hide; Coconut would probably talk himself into trouble. The ensign would assure the officers, and then the talk would usually turn to the A's or the Giants before the ensign went back inside and made good on his promise.

Duty on the aircraft carrier turned out to be a keen fit for the ensign. Aircraft carriers have five thousand people or so onboard—many of them young officers; it's a ready-made party community. Unlike smaller ships, the senior officers could seem a long, long way away. It was a boatload of twenty-somethings with virtually no adult supervision. The cynicism telling the ensign that college was irrelevant followed him to the West Coast after graduation and commissioning as a naval officer—both of which proved very close calls right up to the ceremony dates. Play the game, he told himself, then have a beer.

At this point in his life, it was time to act like a grownup and it wasn't happening. This particular ship developed a very tight swarm of revelers. If they were not massing at the local officers club or nearest Bay-area bar, they would fire up the goings-on at someone's rented house. The San Leandro home base was exploited early and often. The scheme was simple: provide the Jet Fuel and music, get a lot of people there, and then see what happened. Ah, youth! Make *something* happen. A dull time was a greater sin than a bad time.

On that particular night, the ensign and his cohorts called all of the usual suspects to a Make-Something-Happen crusade that they had signed onto simultaneously. Synchronized abandon. Make sure that there was something to re-live tomorrow and the next day, and perhaps all through the upcoming Far East cruise. The Padre started early: he was tripping. He felt compelled to bless everyone, multiple times. This was the sign that the party was starting.

Every one of their parties had a party annex in the driveway. One lieutenant, a self-labeled cowboy who called himself the Country Gentleman, would pull up in his customized full-size van and regale whoever would listen with stories of the Colorado Rockies from which he hailed. Jet Fuel was not for him; it had to be Coors, and everyone knew he kept a full fridge in the back of the van. *"Coors, ain't no downstream beer, ain't no city beer. Coors."* He aped the advertising slogan whenever he reached for another from the fridge. The van always remained in the driveway all night.

An occasional participant was the Snow Queen, so-called because nobody knew her real name, as well as for her taste for powder cocaine. Nobody knew why she came by—that is, nobody knew who met her and brought her into the klatch. She just appeared sometimes, whether it was in the East Bay, the City by the Bay, or Sausalito. Tonight, she had some of the air wing officers doing lines in one of the bedrooms. They came back out to the party thinking that things were moving in slow motion. They joined The Padre on his sacred mission, and it became their calling to speed things up. Boost the bass! Rally the dancers! Toss an amp through the wall! Leap off the roof into the lemon trees!

The Country Gentleman did not allow the Snow Queen anywhere near his van. He knew what she brought to the party, and in his mind it was blasphemous. Rocky Mountain beer and good American fun—*that* was right.

At some point in the evening, Coconut and the ensign, totally fried, were staring at a table leg for an indeterminate length of time. Then, as though experiencing simultaneous revelations, they nodded to each other, arose, and began walking down the street to Church's Fried Chicken.

The two virtually held each other up, forming a walking upside down 'V' as they traversed the dimly-lit neighborhood. It was a working class community and by this time of night it was quiet. The kids were inside; the living room lights up and down the street were going off one-by-one.

The ensign addressed Coconut in what he thought was a whisper. It wasn't.

Coconut shushed him in mid-chuckle.

"Why are you going to eat chicken with me, bozo. The Navigator's daughter—what's her name? Karen? She was was looking at you, my friend. Couldn't you see that?" This seemed to be news to Coconut.

"Hell, yeah. She wants me, she wants all of me, she wants to have my children is what *she* wants!"

"Now you're just being a prick." The ensign stumbled into a low-hanging branch and swatted it away. "Anyway, if you know she wants you, why did you leave?"

"What if I can't help myself?" Coconut had a serious expression, as though now they were talking about something that mattered. "As drunk as I am, she'd probably have her way with me. I can't take that chance." His eyes opened wide, as though he had just said something akin to a state secret.

"Seriously?"

"But you, you saved my ass again."

"Again? When did I save your ass before?"

"Remember when you showed up at the house a couple

months ago after you'd been in the city? I was with that tall girl—Jess, Jules, something with a 'J'."

"Jennifer, from the Club. Yeah, I remember. You came running out of your bedroom yelling for me to rescue you. 'Help me, Help me!' You looked like an idiot."

"No shit, one more beer or ten more minutes and I would've failed the Lord."

"I didn't do anything, I just walked in."

"I told her we were gay and that she'd better run or you'd kill us both."

"And she bought that?"

"She was trying to run wasn't she?" insisted Coconut. "Not such a good idea in heels, but, really, she was trying to run."

"You're full of shit."

"You saved me! If I ever decide to give it up it'll be to you!"

"You need to tone that down or they're gonna toss us both out of This Man's Navy."

"Seriously, you just keep watching out for my butt."

The ensign motioned Coconut to quiet down. "Besides, if you keep finding girls like Jennifer, I might not be strong enough to save you. Damn, she was built… I mean *built* built." He flexed, in a Hulk-comic-book-character kind of way.

Coconut halted, and then wrinkled his brow in thought. "Hey, wait a minute! Why are you going with me for chicken when we've got a houseful of women?" His eyes opened wide, and he continued walking. "You're pining again, aren't you? Are you pining?"

"Just not in the mood tonight, that's all."

You know that Miss Alison is not gonna wait, don't you? She's hot and somebody's gonna have her and it won't be you."

"You've never met her. How do you know she's hot?"

"She must be, or you wouldn't disappoint every girl who pays you any attention. Like what's-her-name—Annie—over in Walnut Creek. I mean, would you? In fact..."Coconut strained to regain his train of thought. "Alison is perfect."

"Maybe." In fact, he thought she might be.

"Then she's definitely out of your league. And so what? Annie's more your type anyway."

"How would you know my...?"

"What's-her-name—Annie—is sweet and modest and hiding some awesome hotness and God I'm hungry."

As they approached the parking lot, the bright lights of Church's caused the ensign and Coconut to shield their eyes. Coconut continued: "Well, maybe I can't rescue you from perfect, but you can keep saving me for my Calling." He raised his voice and put his hand to his heart, "My hero!"

"My hero!" A feigned squeaky voice mocked Coconut.

The drunken pair turned to see two bikers leaning on their motorcycles. They were middle-aged, both graying, with their hair pulled back in pony tails. One was thin and his faced lined hard with age. The other was a big man, grossly overweight. His torn leather jacket was too small, and the insignia it contained was faded and illegible. His face was spotted and pale.

"My hero!" the big man repeated. Then, for the benefit of his companion, "Faggots."

Coconut turned toward the pair and yelled, "Eat shit and die!"

Immediately the ensign put his hand out in a stop sign toward the bikers and said, "Whoa, whoa! He's a drunk virgin, don't listen to him. You can't take him serious. Really, he doesn't mean anything."

"A virgin, eh?" The big man looked at his skinny friend and said, "We can do something about that, can't we?"

As the two bikers scornfully laughed, the ensign shoved Coconut into the restaurant and the two plopped down in a red linoleum booth for four. Coconut's sermon still ate at the ensign.

"As long as I demand perfection in a wife, and perfection isn't exactly throwing herself my way, I'm free to sample the wares... right? I can be like a butterfly, going from flower to flower. Hey, maybe that should be my nickname—'Butterfly'."

"'Butterfly'? Seriously?" He leaned across the table and whispered, "You know what that term means, don't you? The oldtimers say the Filipino hookers will cut your throat for calling yourself that."

Seated at a nearby table were two women. One was pretty—very pretty. Lines under her eyes and a little extra weight said *middle age* but her perfect smile and bright face said *wow!* The alcohol amped up the image.

She looked at the ensign. "I've seen you here before." And then immediately, "Who's your friend?"

"The girls call him Coconut. I call him asshole. Take your pick."

She slid in next to Coconut.

The ensign warned, "Beware, he's a virgin and is fiercely guarding his honor!"

"Ohhh," she cooed.

Coconut leaned across the table to the ensign, and in a drunken whisper implored, "I-can-not-stay-here!"

Coconut and the ensign were quiet on the way home, Coconut's honor firmly intact. Almost in tears, he said, "You did it again, you saved me."

Truth be told, what saved him was when the ensign took out a condom and the two of them used it to play tabletop football. The women had quickly disappeared. Immaturity, it turned out, was an effective form of contraception.

By the time they arrived back at the house, it was late-late. Coconut fell forward until he reached his room. The ensign stepped over a couple casualties passed out in the doorways and entered the kitchen. He tried to take stock: did something noteworthy happen? The answers would have to wait until tomorrow, when the stories began and it was noted who came dragging out of the bedrooms. For the ensign, the party was just another Saturday: got hammered, ate.

A familiar sound pierced the now-quiet night. It was Moose, and he was bellowing. Moose was a big fellow, a former Division I football tight end, from Miami University—not The U—the one in Ohio. When he got tanked, he enjoyed hoisting people. He did this once on a late watch out at sea. He had a messenger hanging by his feet. Fortunately, none of the senior officers smelled anything on his breath or made the connection between Moose drinking and Moose hoisting.

The ensign walked out the front door. Standing under a street light, Moose was holding one of the guests above his head and roaring, as if a victorious silverback claiming supremacy. His victim looked like he might throw up. The ensign coaxed both back into the house, finally convincing Moose that nobody wanted the cops to come.

Inside, Moose and his victim moved on. They sat on a coach, slamming Cheetos and staring at the television's test pattern.

The ensign saw that the screen door to the back yard was off its hinges. He lifted it and pushed it aside, and walked into the back yard. He pulled a lawn chair onto the patio and sat down. It was quiet, a pleasant suburban calm. He now had a chance to think. As usual, his thoughts turned to Alison. Maybe Coconut was right. Maybe he *did* pine for her.

As he did often, he thought back to the sun-bathed Sunday afternoon when he met Alison. It was at the turtle races. Really, he reminded himself, that was a real thing. He was by himself, at a waterside bar in Sausalito, administering some of the hair of the dog following a pretty typical Saturday night. She was with some business colleagues, wasting some time before heading to the airport later that evening. Both were cheering on their chosen turtles.

The participants paid for the privilege of backing any one of the competing turtles. The winners received prizes, such as free drinks or stuffed turtles. The ensign noticed the beautiful girl with the stunning smile and a real aversion to losing. And she was beautiful: Olivia Newton John in "Grease," Jill Clayburgh in "An Unmarried Woman," and Corrine Clery in "Moonraker" all-in-one.

He noticed that the more she lost, the more determined she became. The more determined, the prettier she became. After a while, her vital interest was to beat the ensign. Race after race, his turtle defeated her turtle. Race after race, she moved closer and closer to him. She was disappointed when the turtle races ended for the day. But taking it in stride, she invited the ensign for a drink, to toast his mastery at picking faster turtles. He thought, Now there's the basis of a long-lasting relationship: picking winning turtles.

Shortly after the two contestants settled into chairs on the deck, her pager went off. Alison's group's itinerary changed, and they had to pick up an earlier flight.

Alison, as it turned out, was a lawyer for a Charlotte investment firm. She traveled often, and the two promised to meet on her next trip to the West Coast, and they did. They managed a very pleasant dinner along the water in Berkeley on one of her lay-overs. The next time, they had a couple drinks near the airport, but her colleagues were along.

He couldn't help but think that their first encounter was The Moment, and that perhaps they would never get it back. She wrote a few letters, making him promise that they would meet again in Sausalito for a rematch of the running of the turtles. The last was weeks ago.

Their phone conversations, though brief, were pleasant enough. At their rare dinner dates, he did notice certain points in the conversation that elicited a pursed-lip expression and a "hmm": when he described his friends and their weekend benders; when he talked about his post-Navy career possibilities (for instance,"playing a guitar on a Berkeley street corner, if I can fight off the other troubadors"); and when he told her he was soon going to sea for eight or nine months.

The trials of a long-distance relationship aside, he tried not to bore the party guests with his self-pity. Hell—if she lived next door, she wouldn't come to these gatherings. She'd probably make that face again.

That she was not close by was probably fortuitous. The Navy gave him license to stay an adolescent—and in a way, so did she. Since she was The One, he wasn't going to get serious with anyone else. And then, one day, in the vague but certain future, when the time was right...

Until then, he'd bide his time. He could hook up with those West Coast women as opportunities arose. They might not be perfect like Alison, but they'd do fine. Annie was one of those West Coast women, and she'd more than do. So she wasn't a jet-setting lawyer, rather a marketing major from a party school. But then, so was he!

Was it just coincidence that, over a period of months, Annie kept showing up at their parties? Was he that dense? Was she—? Ridiculous! Coconut was just getting into his head.

C'mon, where was that peanut butter?

*

*

*   *

*

He thought back to a port visit early in the ship's western Pacific cruise. The ship was tied up at the Subic Bay naval station. Adjacent was Olongapo City, Republic of the Philippine Islands. For the shipboard partiers, same goals, different smells. The carrier tied up at the sprawling naval base at Subic Bay several times during their long deployment. Sailors quickly chose certain bars in town as their own home bases away from home.

Across Shit River and down the mud-covered roads into town, some of the ship's officers had gone to Mama-san's place for some *mojo* and San Miguel. The creaking ceiling fans only faintly dispelled the oppressive humidity. The music—

American country and rock music sung by Filipinos playing imitation instruments—was loud, and smoke hung thickly.

"I love you, no shit. Buy me champagne cocktail?" The prostitutes were smiling and bouncy, masking a desperation born of poverty and rejection, and looking to survive in a business that was not at all light. One night's service to a serviceman, at a few pesos, meant for these women rice and squid for their families.

Mama-san watched over the goings-on. Nobody knew her age; she could be seventy, or the thirty-five year old veteran of a tough life. Her girls had either been sold to her from desperate families in the countryside, or she had rescued them from the gutters. Some had been with her for a few weeks, others for a several years.

The afternoon sun was bright, but harsh. The air was visible, such that one could see the waves of heat oscillating ahead.

The ensign crossed Shit River, tossing a peso to a girl on a bonka boat as he went. There were always children in the fleet of skinny boats floating below the bridge. The girls were dressed in colorful traditional dress and held wire baskets with which to catch pesos. The boys were prepared to dive for pesos. That was unfortunate: Shit River wasn't really a river. It was a drainage ditch.

The ensign moved quickly up Magsaysay Boulevard. It had been a long day. He and Coconut had spent it in one of the engine rooms as sailors were repairing a pump. It was a hundred ten degrees in the bowels of the ship, and men were sweating rivers as they rotated in and out of the space to keep from passing out; ten minutes was the most a man could remain safely.

Though he and Coconut never touched a tool, they monitored the work and encouraged the workers. They took turns reporting to the senior officers who kept asking for updates.

When the pump was declared ready to go, Coconut was nowhere to be found. The ensign showered and left the ship, figuring that Coconut collapsed into sleep. Who could blame him? But when he arrived at Mama-san's, Coconut was sitting with Dori, one of Mama-san's ladies, and sucking on a San Miguel. Dori's age was undeterminable—she could have been twenty or thirty. Or forty, for that matter. She was attractive and shapely, big-busted for a Filipino. She had chosen Coconut the first time she saw him. She intended to marry him and come to the U.S. as a Navy wife. That he was a virgin was added incentive. If she could be his first, she could possibly be his first love. And that could be the ticket to the magical mystical place she had heard so many stories about, called California.

Tonight, Dori decided to reel in the big fish. She figured she had let out enough line.

"Coconut, you know it time. You know what I have for you? You won't be sorry."

Coconut was blushing. He was embarrassed that he was embarrassed.

The elusive First Time had become a spectator sport. Men and women were having conversations around the room, but always with one ear tuned to Dori and Coconut.

"I show you good time, all your friends be jealous."

"How do I know I won't get some disease?"

"Oh no! I for you only. No one else. Clean as virgin, you see." This conversation had happened before.

Gender-based teams had formed around the sport. The

men cheered on Coconut, trying to convince him to give in. The ladies' team brainstormed to come up with new ways to convince Coconut to sample the Apple. As the conversation grew louder, Dori stood behind Coconut's barstool and leaned against him.

"You know important people, commanders even? They want me. I wait for you only. No money, no make love. Wait for you. You number one." There was a whiff of desperation in her tone. She grabbed a handful of Coconut's shirt sleeve.

Coconut's face began to change. He felt a tension that was not there before. "Look, I may head back to the ship early. I have a lot of work..."

All heads turned following a sudden spate of yelling in Filipino. Coconut went flying from the barstool into the near wall. His eyes showed shock. Dori had clearly freaked. Her eyes were shark eyes, black and unthinking. She dropped to the floor, straddling Coconut and clutching the front of his shirt, butterfly knifepoint against his neck. She didn't speak; she shook. Coconut tried to slide up the wall, pushing with his hands. Dori followed his motion, her grip firm and the knife at his throat.

Mama-san walked toward them. "Dori, no, Dori," she pleaded. She switched to Filipino, imploring Dori to calm down and re-think. The Navy men and the hookers flowed slowly into a semi-circle around the altercation. Nobody knew if Dori was capable of following through with the attack, but nobody wanted to test her. Eyes were downcast as calming words floated from those gathered. Everyone got quieter and quieter until the only remaining sound was Dori's tortured breathing.

It was as though the air pressure changed. The room felt

heavy. Men used to reacting to emergencies were slowing down time in their minds, performing the calculus of probable results. What to do next?

Then, in the night, a man bellowed. People looked up, eyes wide. The wall behind Dori and Coconut exploded. Chunks of faux adobe burst into a thousand fragments as the room filled with white dust. Dori was on her back, the knife six or eight feet beyond. The Padre quickly picked it up and backed away. Coconut was knocked over, and then, looking to escape, got up and scampered toward an open window. He managed to lock glances with the ensign, and muttered, "I-can-not-stay-here!"

Coconut grabbed the iron frame of the window and swung out into the night: that it was a second-story window didn't enter his thinking. He landed on the awning below, rolled off, slowed his progress by grabbing the edge of the awning, and dropped to the street.

He sprinted back to the ship through the steamy, seamy, half-lit streets. He never returned to Olongapo City.

Moose stood up in the middle of the room, swatting the drywall dust off of his clothes. He had seen the goings-on from the back room through a casement window. In the quiet, he had decided to save Coconut, silently sneaking around to the side of the wall opposite the hostage-taking. Then he burst through the wall as though it was an opposing lineman.

As several of the girls pulled Dori into the backroom, Mama-san announced that the bar would be closing early. She thought she should lower her profile, since her establishment would be in danger from the local authorities if word got out.

Throughout the tumult, a woman by the name of Belle had snuggled closer and closer to the ensign. He knew who she was but had not seen her very often at the bar. He presumed she had an exclusive boyfriend, or else had somehow left the profession; some girls managed to do that if they knew accounting or had some personal or business connections.

As Mama-san and some of the girls cleaned up the room, the ensign realized he didn't want to go back to the ship. In President Marcos' Philippines there was a midnight curfew for American servicemen, so plans and deals had to be made before then. If he didn't move quickly, Belle might leave.

Belle was a beauty—stylish, and quiet, but not remote. The ensign figured this could be a perfect arrangement for the remainder of the cruise—Belle as his kept woman. They made small talk, then a decision.

He thought about Alison. The booze shortened the consideration. Besides, when was her last letter? He couldn't remember. Sure, he was in love with her, but it wasn't going to happen, so what harm would there be in a little strange so far away from The World?

He surprised himself by wondering if what's-her-name-Annie would be hurt by this. The line of thought was trumped by *mojo* and proximity.

The ensign and Belle left the bar together. The custom was for the man to pay a "bar fine" to the mama-san, allowing the woman to leave. With all of tonight's commotion, he would have to pay the bar fine later. As they made their way down side streets, a boy, maybe 12 years old, with a green Motley Crew tee-shirt, came up to Belle, speaking Filipino. He sounded as though he was chiding her. The ensign was annoyed—Belle was angry.

"It's none of your business!" she yelled in English. Then she yelled some more in Filipino.

The boy continued his picking.

"He doesn't need to know!"

More yelling ensued.

The boy suddenly lunged at the ensign, who instinctively guarded his wallet and fended him off. Belle screamed angrily and the boy ran.

Ten minutes later, at the entrance to Belle's hovel, a sailor stood, seething, jaw set.

"You bitch! I see it now. You found yourself an officer." His face was red, and he spat out, "More money for the whore!"

"You go," Belle commanded. The outlines of two men appeared and slid closer, still in the shadows. The sailor realized what was happening.

The ensign did not defend Belle. He didn't know what he would be defending her for. The sailor never looked directly at him, but turned and stormed off, muttering, "You can have her, if you can afford her."

As Belle and the ensign entered the small house, they walked through the dark entry way into a brightly-lit kitchen. As if on cue, food appeared on the linoleum-surfaced table, and plastic-coated chairs were pulled up. Ice-cold San Miguels appeared. The shadows from outside showed themselves, opening beers and smiling. The more outgoing one turned a huge smile toward the ensign and introduced himself as Luzano. Music from a small boombox began to play. Belle and the men, joined by some boys and girls, ate and talked, sometimes in Filipino, sometimes in English.

In a side conversation, Belle and the ensign agreed on terms: as long as he would keep the household in groceries, Belle was his. Certainly that night was his—food, plenty of beer, music and laughter. Later, after the younger ones disappeared and then the adults excused themselves, Belle and the ensign moved to a small room in the back. There was a prettily-made mattress on the floor, surrounded by small stands with knick-knacks. Most of these had religious connections. The weak overhead light actually added to the romance of the place, when it might have been expected to reveal the sleeziness of the arrangement.

There was no discounting Belle's beauty. Silhouetted against the overhead light, she created a stunning erotic image. Perhaps it should have shown itself for the tawdry situation it was. But that is not how Belle and the ensign lived it, into the early hours.

The next evening, and for many after, the ensign sidestepped the bar and went straight to Belle's. He and Luzano would have a couple of beers before Belle would appear. Luzano loved American movies and was a big Yankees fan, and they could talk films and baseball for hours. When Belle came into the kitchen, she and the ensign would proceed to carry out their domestic lives together.

When the ensign's duty night came along, when he was required to remain onboard the ship to run the engineering plant overnight, he shocked himself by worrying about Belle. Would she find someone else? Someone with more money? A senior officer? Would he also end up standing at her door as she escorted a commander into her home? Would Luzano be ready to beat the shit out of him if he made a fuss?

The day before the ship was to leave on a long voyage into the Indian Ocean, the ensign once more crossed Shit River on his way to Belle's. There was a commotion alongside the city-side of the drainage ditch. He could see the bloated body of a young boy on a gurney. There were strips of flesh missing from his mostly declothed back. A green tee-shirt collar remained around his neck. Recognizing one of the Shore Patrol, a sailor he knew who was on loan from the ship, he made his way closer to the gurney.

"What the hell happened, Mac?"

Petty Officer McElroy recognized the ensign, even though he worked in another division on the ship. He had heard the ensign was an upright guy, and so he volunteered what he knew about the situation.

"Sir, seems like this kid was harassing customers, and the local police beat him with a hose. We don't know if he was beaten to death and thrown in Shit River, or beaten and thrown into the water where he drowned."

"Who is he?"

"Looks like he's been in Shit River for some time, but there are no reports of missing kids. I bet we never find out."

The ensign, instead of turning right to Belle's, turned left to Mama-san's. He had some *mojo* and went back to the ship early.

*

*

*

*

*

*

*

*

Presently, it was four thirty in the morning, in the South China Sea, heading back to the Philippines. The ensign moved with great ease from the ship's bow to the superstructure and up to the charthouse.

It was startime, that sliver of time just before dawn or just after sunset when the brightest stars—those best for shooting—were visible, along with a stark horizon. For thousands of years, it has been known by mariners as that window through which they could find out where they were.

"Good morning, Master Chief, I am ready.

"I know you are, sir."

"Are you ready to make port tomorrow, Master Chief?"

"Doesn't make any difference to me, sir, I took everyone's duty, so I will be onboard until we arrive stateside."

"Even after a hundred days, you don't want to run off this ship?" the ensign asked with some incredulity.

"No sir. When we get to California I will have a different answer."

"Let's do this. Where's the quartermaster?"

"I told him that I would take the marks for you this morning. He's been working hard—I told him to get a little extra sleep."

The Master Chief called out the time and the ensign smoothly swung the sextant and called out the readings for each star. In minutes the two were in the charthouse, punching the calculations and plotting the lines.

15° 13' 55" north, 118° 31' east. Yessir! That's where the ship was, exactly.

Later that morning, land was sighted. The ship made its way into the channel approaching Subic Bay. A harbor pilot boarded the ship from a port control launch for the final approach to the pier, which the ship made with the assistance of two tugs.

Men had talked all night about the great feats of drinking and amazing sexual exploits that would happen when the ship tied up. Shortly after the brows connecting ship to pier went over, there was a mass exodus of sailors onto the base, across Shit River and down Magsaysay. A great cloud of dust hung over the entire area.

But after months at sea, tolerance for the booze was way down, as was staying time. By noon the town was as quiet as one would ever see it.

The ensign remained onboard, working on the details for the voyage home.

A couple days later The Padre invited the ensign and several others to a party he had arranged on a local island resort. They took a launch to the island, where the officers played golf, had some San Miguel, and checked into their Quonset huts. There were plenty of hookers on hand. The Padre had arranged several for his friends, and he introduced Neema to the ensign.

As the sun went down, the officers sat by a stone grill, eating steaks and grilled corn. Each woman would fetch beers for her man and fill his plate for him. Neema cut the ensign's porterhouse and fed him. She even held and turned the corn as the he ate it. She would occasionally look to one of the older women, silently inquiring as to what to do. A terse reply in Filipino would follow.

The men basked in the luxury. "War is hell," one offered.

But on this day the ensign was thinking another way.

"Bill, how old is she?" he whispered to his friend.

"Prime, baby, she's definitely a virgin."

"But how old?"

"I think Mama-san said she was fifteen," The Padre replied dismissively.

The ensign got up, handed The Padre some money, and walked away. Danwell looked confused: how does somebody turn this down? The ensign slipped Neema some money and headed for the boat dock. Under his breath he said, "I-can-not-stay-here!"

But he could have stayed. He thought about the worlds he could be sucked into without much effort. He could be pulled into an upscale world in high-end Charlotte or wealthy San Francisco and think it normal. He could be pulled into the daily existence off Magsaysay and think it normal. He considered how easily he could have stayed in the world of the whores near a naval base in the Philippines—a world of victims, in a system he didn't create but of which he was a part. He could have told himself that they didn't look like victims. People everywhere do what they have to to put food on the table, and he was providing, right?

But maybe, he thought, he would consciously choose a world that felt right and righteous.

He took a launch back to his ship. His first thought as he contemplated a change in direction was not Alison. He took a breath and headed to his office. He had work to do, and a call to make.

Pittman Forge

By David W. Brooks

The reporter turned to see where the stringer was pointing. When he saw the girl leaning against the wall, he felt suddenly dizzy, almost nauseous. It was as though he was trying to look at two things at once, one with each eye, and merge them together in his mind. "You mean the one in the Florida t-shirt? You're sure?"

"Yes. Why, what's wrong?"

"Nothing." The reporter looked a moment longer until the nausea passed; when he turned back around it felt to him as if everything but the stringer had changed. He didn't know what the change was, could not explain it, but it struck him like a body blow. As the stringer continued to talk about the trial, the reporter scanned the room, his eyes moving slowly, overwhelmed by a million things shouting for attention. There were so many, he didn't know where to look or what to consider first, and he felt lost and uncertain in a way he'd never been before, not even when he had stepped into Annie's for the first time the previous evening.

Annie's was exactly how he had supposed a small-town restaurant would be—calendars on the walls, country music on the juke-box, a fat waitress who knew everybody by name, and even a Blue Plate Special served on a blue-trimmed plate. Being a stranger, he hadn't felt completely comfortable there, but nothing had surprised him.

In fact, nothing in Jackson County surprised him, even though it was his first visit to coal country. Although he had been a reporter at the Guardian for six years, this was his first trip from the capital to the edge of the state—an area he had known only through black-and-white photos of tar-paper shacks that the newspaper ran in its annual finger-shaking stories on poverty.

As soon as he had begun to rise into the foothills, leaving the shiny, new four-lane highway that had been named for some deceased congressman and turning onto a two-lane road known only by its state highway number, things had looked the way he thought they would. There had been the decrepit pasted-together houses; the gashes left by the surface mines that hopped from hillside to hillside, tracing the coal seams; the sudden darkness on the morning road when it cut through the steep V of a hollow. And there were the people—poor, pasty-faced, with bad posture and ill-matched clothing, shuffling along in the weeds at the side of the road or sitting, suspicious and mean, on their porches and in their pick-ups.

Pittman Forge, the county's only town of any size, had also been as he expected: long and narrow, clinging to the main street as if afraid to let go, constructed like a bell curve with shanty housing and mobile homes at each end. These slowly gave way to larger houses towards the middle of town and the business district in the center: a few two-story brick buildings, many shut with boarded windows, and a single stop-light where the county courthouse, Baptist Church and Miner's Bank studied each other.

Officially he was there to help fill the paper's pages during a slow news summer by covering a murder trial—but he had taken on the assignment in order to gather pictures of rural mountain life that could be slipped to readers over morning coffee in subdivisions and apartments—pictures to let them feel that they understood the plight of the mountain poor; a quick guilt fix to start them on their busy business day. Now having seen the town and its surroundings, it seemed to him that he needn't have made the trip; that he could have assembled the whole thing in his head at the office from a thousand memories of things read and heard. "It's a living cliché," he told his editor when he called in to the office the first evening.

"Clichés have to be based on something," the editor told him back. "So what's your story looking like?"

"Just what the stringer told us—nice girl goes bonkers over husband lured from home by man-eater and shoots him."

"No verdict yet?"

"No. They'll only get through the prosecution today, if that. It took the whole morning to pick the jurors—everybody here knows everybody else. Impartial souls were hard to find."

"That's good; mention that in the story." The editor was always quick to pounce on the obvious and claim it as his own. "Can you give me thirty inches?"

"Sure. There's lots of small-town-life stuff to put in."

"Good boy." The sound of the editor's pencil scratch on the budget sheet came over the phone. "I like you wordy collegiate-types in the summertime. What's the schedule look like tomorrow?"

"Defense will probably take up the morning—with arguments and instructions, it should go to the jury after lunch."

"Think they'll convict her?"

"My guess is they'll do the usual: drop it to involuntary manslaughter—there's no argument that she shot him—so they can find her guilty and the judge can give her probation due to extenuating circumstances. Then everybody gets to feel good about serving justice without actually putting a local girl behind bars."

The editor grunted. "Well, plan on coming back tomorrow when it goes to the jury; the stringer can call in the verdict. We don't want to spend another night's hotel money if we don't have to. Got it?"

"Whatever you say. It breaks my heart, of course, only getting one night to wander the streets of Pittman Forge."

"Streets?"

"There's three of them."

The editor laughed—he was always careful to laugh at a joke. "Don't turn into a mountain man on us, now," he warned.

After hanging up, the reporter plugged in his word processor and wrote his story. Although he hadn't been on the court beat for years, it went easily: he found trials simple to cover, with set characters, an established ritual, and a clear-cut result—like a football game or election. He pulled a large part of the material from the notes he had jotted down during the day. Most of it came from neighbors of the young couple, who had lived in a run-down-but-neat house on one of the town's few back streets. Everyone he talked to had praised the pair—especially the wife—describing her as a lively, pretty girl unfazed by the couple's money problems. The praise had been more mixed for the husband, a bit of a hell-raiser in high school who had settled down to become a model member of the community, until he began seeing another woman shortly before the shooting. None of the people he interviewed were willing to talk about his indiscretion, and the reporter was left to build a shadowy picture of the interloper. He envisioned her in a black dress and pearls; a wealthy, bored, attractive woman approaching middle age who was seeking both occasional sex and companionship; in control and amusing herself with the younger man. All of the neighbors did agree that the marriage had seemed a happy one, and that the infidelity, which had quickly become common knowledge in the town, was puzzling. Perhaps, they suggested, the scarcity of work had gotten to him.

At McGinnis Mine No. 7, a company vice-president exhibiting the industry's hard-learned suspicion of the press, described the murdered man as a good worker who had wanted to be a miner like his uncle.

"He'd been working just part-time lately, correct?"

"Reduced shifts," the vice-president corrected, though without satisfaction, as if the words were forced on him. He looked away from the reporter to a map of the mines: incomprehensibly intricate lines and angles documenting where the innards of the mountain had been hauled out. "Hell, damn business ain't been worth jack-shit for two years now— everybody's on reduced shifts. Except those of us trying to sell the damn stuff. Took a yearly order for three hundred tons last week—three hundred!—and I was glad for it. Used to be I wouldn't spit on an order like that—now it makes me go home and have a beer." He looked back at the reporter, who was trying to write unobtrusively, a trick he had never mastered. "Anything else?"

"No, I don't think so. Thank you for your help."

The vice-president watched him with stony eyes until he had exited the mine.

In the afternoon, the reporter went to the trial and was snagged by the stringer—a high school senior who received a nominal fee from UPI for providing scores of regional games and local election vote totals, and who had provided the paper with background information on the trial. The two sat together in the spectator section with a clear view of the defendant, who sat quiet and demure in her chair listening to opening arguments. The prosecutor spent his time hammering on the gruesome details of the shooting, waving pictures of the corpse that he planned to introduce as evidence. The round-ribbed defense attorney told the jury that he would prove the crime to be a case of a young girl driven to make a terrible mistake by circumstances beyond her control, overwhelmed by the fear of losing the man who had been her grade-school sweetheart. Lurking behind his words, but never brought to the fore, was the woman who had tempted the husband away. The reporter was disappointed to find that she wasn't on the witness list, and he asked the stringer about it over dinner at Annie's.

"I-I don't know," the boy stammered, reluctant to admit uncertainty in front of a man he saw as a possible key to his future. "She stays on the fringe of things. A lot of people don't like her."

"Had she known him a long time? Or his wife?"

"Sure, I guess. Everybody did. Everybody knows everybody."

"Does she like it here?"

The stringer gave an uncomfortable shrug. "I don't know."

"Does she want to get away, do you think?"

"Who doesn't?"

The picture he had built since arriving in the town stayed in his mind: a woman born for the city but locked in the mountains by circumstance, who in desperation acted out her libidinous fantasies with the man and took out her frustration on the couple. It was a pasteboard picture, something from a soap opera, but he knew it would do for the article.

Which it did. He was able to shuffle things to hide the identity of the woman by emphasizing the small-town upbringing of the defendant, the closeness of the community and its shock when it learned of the killing. He spent several paragraphs describing how the girl had sat on the front porch with her husband's shotgun, waiting for him to come home from his tryst with the older woman, and then fired the left barrel into his chest as he stepped up from the yard, the blast flinging him backwards off the porch. When the sheriff's cars arrived, the wife was sitting expressionless on the swing: the gun, still half-loaded, lay on the porch where she had dropped it and the husband was growing cold on the front lawn.

He ended the story with a description of the hard economic times that had hit the coal fields, and some conjecture about the effect this had on the town and townspeople. The reporter finished the story a half-hour before his deadline and sent it over the modem to the office. Afterward, unwilling to sit idle in the uncomfortable room, he went for a walk in the clear, warm night.

Most of Pittman Forge was closed and dark, with only a scattering of street lights working. Even Annie's was dark, though it was only a little after 8 p.m. He wandered into the center of town and was attracted to the glow and noise that emanated from the small Piggly Wiggly supermarket, still open, its parking lot half-full of people and cars. Standing at the edge of the light he saw that there were two separate groups: a few adults holding fat brown grocery bags doing their shopping, entering and exiting slowly from the store; and a small crowd of younger people collected at the far edge of the lot because there was nowhere else to go.

The young crowd was centered on a trio of two men and a teenaged girl; the men wearing camouflage jackets and jeans and combat boots, the girl in a black tube top and bare feet. He could hear a few words of their conversation but not enough to follow it; at one point the woman began to laugh, a loud scream with her head thrown back, and she staggered about— whether from drunkenness or hilarity he couldn't tell— slapping both camouflaged men on their shoulders. The rest of the teenagers became more animated at this performance. It was as if the girl's sudden burst of energy had also energized them, but after a moment the crowd had settled back down, with the woman reclining on her elbows on the hood of an orange Pinto, feet dangling carelessly over the grill, the men leaning on either side of her.

The reporter was unexpectedly stung by a depressing sense of fatalism. All of the participants—the shoppers and the partiers—appeared trapped to him. Their choreographed routine seemed so inculcated by the town and the mountains that, even had they escaped from this monotony to the cities, they would have had to return, for they could never fit in anywhere else.

Burdened with this melancholy, he left the lights and walked into the deeper darkness of the residential area, where dim forms could be sensed on the porches and occasional lights filtered through curtains in front windows. He walked until the sidewalk disappeared and then turned around; on the journey back, someone across the unlit street murmured 'hello'. Surprised, he nodded in return. The Piggly Wiggly parking lot was empty when he passed it again.

The next morning began with the defense case, which was disappointing: an endless parade of character witnesses attesting to the moral rectitude and happy, amicable nature of the defendant, who sat and listened without reaction. Her family, her teachers, her minister, and her friends all took their place in the box and attested how wonderful she had always been, how sweet and charming and friendly—until the past few months. The attorney, his fat face sweating hard, his hands going back to the piles of paper on his table as if for refuge, cut them off at that point, never allowing them to go into what had changed her. On the surface this was done to avoid hearsay testimony—but the reporter realized that the attorney was banking on imagination being stronger than recitation. By allowing the jury members to complete the tale themselves, they would paint in the details of the story from their own suppositions rather than a neighbor's halting phrases.

And it worked: even the reporter, who saw what the attorney was doing, began to imagine a happy marriage eaten away by an evil like a cancer, a monstrous infidelity that crushed a woman's spirit and left her nothing but the shotgun in the closet. As tale compounded tale, the picture grew to epic proportions—a bloated, heinous creature of fate beyond the clinical reach of the courts or of law, and even the prosecutor's frantic efforts in closing arguments could not pierce it.

By lunchtime, the jury had been instructed and led away to their little room. The reporter, convinced that deliberations would not take long, decided to wait a while before starting the four-hour drive back to the capital, since it would be easier to wind things up in person. With the stringer tagging along, the reporter once again and crossed the street to Annie's, where the two of them took a table and discussed what they had seen. As they talked, the reporter once again mentioned how he wished the home-wrecker had been called to the stand so he could have seen her—it was then that the stringer pointed her out against the wall. The reporter turned, anticipating the visage he had drawn of the seductress: perhaps dressed in scarlet, leisurely smoking a cigarette dangling from a gold and ebony holder casually held between her manicured fingers.

Instead, he found himself looking at the girl from the Piggly Wiggly parking lot, now wearing a pink-speckled Florida t-shirt, laughing as she had done the night before. For an instant his two stereotypes, the sophisticated paramour and the personification of the little coal town, struggled to occupy the same space and his vision wavered, but then both cracked and crumbled from the strain, revealing an image he hadn't built from past associations, and he was left to stare in confusion. It was as if the woman had been forcibly altered, and for the first time he saw details in her face, the tightness of the eyes, her thin lips and sharp chin, not just the style of hair and clothes. For the first time he wondered why she was laughing, what it was that amused her and why she found it funny— how, at this time, she could find anything funny.

He looked at the people around her and tried to figure out their relationships, but could reach no conclusions. The certainty of his beliefs had fled and he felt lost. He had been like a child, accepting things as presented without wondering how they got that way, seeing Pittman Forge as an extension of the flat image he had brought with him and never asking what had made it so, how people had come there and why they stayed. But he could do that no longer. He suddenly realized that the follow-up article would be very difficult to write.

He gazed around the room at the things he had once over-looked. He saw the calendars on the wall—not just inexpensive decoration but one that by its bland practicality avoided the statements and standards of art alien to the area. He listened to the country music—the music which, no matter how plasticized, still made at least a pretense of coming from places and backgrounds important to the town. He saw the fat waitress—her physique a testament to years of work serving diner food.

Only the stringer looked unchanged to him, because he had understood the stringer from the start, had sympathized with the boy's vision of newspaper work as a bright-hued escape and so had seen his persona without effort; everyone else was new, curiously lit from within in ways he could not fathom, possessed with reasons for speech and dress that would take him years to discover. He listened and watched, trying to understand what they were saying and why, tried to put himself in their places, but failed. He didn't know enough about the feelings and pressures of their lives. He could only observe, watching them moving about and talking, leaning on counters, shouting from table to table or eating quietly, and he could only listen to their reactions when it was announced that the jury had come back, could only follow slowly at the rear of the crowd as they stepped out of the restaurant. In the street he had to stop and stare at the mountains jutting up behind the buildings on both sides of him, mountains he had thought of only as adornments, as movie backdrops for a coal town setting. Now he saw that the narrow valley they formed kept Pittman Forge squeezed long and thin—how could he have missed that? For the first time, he saw the town and its people in terms of the land and not the other way around, and the difference staggered him.

He was late getting to the courtroom—even the stringer abandoned him in the middle of the road—and as he came in he was hit by the shocked chatter of the crowd and the stern rumble of the judge imposing the minimum sentence for first-degree murder: life in prison. Automatically the reporter looked at the defendant, who was sitting white-faced, her attorney patting her shoulder, and watched the crowd as it swarmed, still buzzing, past him out of the room. He knew he should have some opinion about the verdict but couldn't formulate his thoughts sufficiently: nothing surprised him anymore. Or perhaps everything did.

People were talking of the verdict as they streamed by him. He heard—or thought he heard—one man say: "I guess you shouldn't shoot people even if you are a charming child." But he didn't try to get reaction statements for his article. He glanced from one person to another, all different, all unknown to him, and he stood helpless, unable break his paralysis, standing silent for long minutes until they had gone and the stringer, confused, sidled up to him.

"Pretty surprising, huh?" the boy ventured, but the reporter could think of nothing to say. He only nodded and made his way slowly out of the courthouse to the street, where he had to stop and look around once more. It was several minutes before he made it to his car for the long drive home.

Poets Out of Time

By Bungalow Stokes

They reveled in puzzles, they wrote in code
I can't deal in Renaissance sonnets
Or read something that begins with 'Ode'
I may sneak a peak from time to time
And see how Ginsburg howled
That just leaves me empty; I am partial to a rhyme

Yeats may stroll London and then try to evoke
A whim some time, he in Innisfree
But Thomas Coram's master stroke
Seeing Fleet Street gin babies dying
And by doing something saved a few
No verse could be a substitute for trying

What do the Joves and Juves and Ulysseses say
Or have to do with my commute
Or taxes or school expenses or my 401K
On these the classics are 100% mute
They make references to long-ago mythical spots
And probably even have those wrong
And none were in my iPod on one of my suburban trots

So where is the poet who can make me smell the fumes
On I-95 as I head north
Or feel the vibrations or hear the booms
Of modern living, or the magazines strewn in living rooms
But mostly where is the poet or two
Who can make us feel of our wars, men "died to make men holy,
Let us die to make men free" as once found the heart, in 1862?

The Day the Sun Went Out

By Asher Roth

I'm sure you remember the day the sun went out.

It was…

Let me start over.

She had left just before dawn, or what would have been the dawn, packing her belongings into two large suitcases, three shoulder bags and several totes, and driving away in the Lexus. No warning, no sign. She left without a sound.

I was asleep. I awoke to the darkness.

Iliana Kovikkova was a concert pianist. Her forte was late 19th Century French composers: Chopin, Ravel, Satie and Debussy. As I discovered, there were many others. I'm sure you've heard Claude Debussy's *Clair De Lune*, one of the movements from his *Suite bergamasque*. It's a lovely piece, intimate and moving even when played by a novice. In Iliana's expert hands it was radiant—every lingering note immaculate, each shimmering passage enveloping you and bathing your soul. At least, that's how it affected me.

I first saw her in the National Gallery of Art, in the French Impressionist wing. She was standing off to my right in the middle of the room, studying a large Monet painting of a garden of sunflowers, and so I first noticed her in profile: dressed all in white, tall and willowy, her blonde hair cascading over her shoulders. A skylight in the center of the ceiling illuminated the room, the sun's rays encircling her like a spotlight. She seemed aglow, almost ethereal.

Now, I don't normally approach strangers in public places, least of all an art gallery, but I was drawn to her as a moth is to a flame. Admittedly, I was physically attracted to her—I mean, she was absolutely gorgeous—but this went far beyond some base carnal craving to a desire to explore this young woman's essence, to learn as much about her as I could, then and there.

"Monet, huh?" I asked her. I wondered if I could have sounded more like a jerk. This was especially true as I was an assistant professor of art history at American University, and my dissertation had been on Renoir, one of Monet's contemporaries. I'm certain that I knew more about Claude Monet than anyone else in that building that Saturday. I knew that the sunflower painting was of Monet's own garden—that he kept gardens as a hobby at each of his homes throughout his life. I knew that this particular portrait was of his house at Vétheuil in 1880, that he was forty years old when he painted it, and that his wife of nine years, Camille Doncieux, had succumbed to tuberculosis only a few months before.

I figured that my awkward introduction had ruined any chance of getting to know this enchanting creature, but to my surprise she responded in kind.

"Yeah, Monet," she nodded and smiled, still gazing at the painting. She had a hint of a northern European accent with the kind of subtle lilt I associated with Scandinavians. I wasn't versed enough to place it, but I guessed it was Swedish. I was close—geographically, at least—I learned later that she was Estonian. She glanced at me with inquisitive, penetrating eyes of cerulean blue. "You like his stuff?"

His "stuff"... a thousand thoughts flashed through my

mind: was she playing a rube to accommodate me, or was she this plebeian? If she had intentionally dumbed down her reply, had she done it out of pity, assuming that I was the rube, or did she perceive that I might be a bit more sophisticated than I had let on and was affording me an opportunity to recover? If the latter, did I now impress her with my knowledge of the artist, or would that come across as pretentious?

I elected to ratchet up my response and gauge her reaction. "Oh, yeah," I nodded back, "he's definitely on my top-ten list of Impressionists. I love the way he facets the light into so many colors."

She looked at the painting as I spoke, then turned back to me and gave another nod. "Yes, that's so true! That's such a good word to describe it—facets. Each of his paintings is like a gemstone to me."

It was my turn to nod. "Yes, exactly! I think that's partly due to his orchestration of the tints and hues. Each dab of paint is like a note, harmonizing into a lovely melody."

Her eyes lit up—I must have struck a chord. "Harmonious hues! Of course!" She extended her hand... the most delicate hand I had ever seen, her fingers long and slender. "My name's Iliana. It's very nice to meet you."

I shook it, a bit less firmly than usual because I didn't want to inadvertently squeeze too hard. No worries there—her grip was stronger and more certain than mine could ever be. "Jacob Redding, and the pleasure is mine," I assured her.

We spent the rest of that afternoon touring the gallery together. She soon learned that I taught art history and she asked for my interpretation of each work we stopped to study. I felt like one of those pocket audio tour guides that museum patrons rent at the information desk, but Iliana didn't seem to mind. I, in turn, took every opportunity to inquire about her, and I soon learned about her very extensive training—a series of music conservatories throughout secondary school and college, all on full scholarship, then Julliard for graduate work and on to the National Symphony Orchestra as a piano soloist.

Having the evening open, she joined me for dinner at La Lumière, a trendy French restaurant I knew in Georgetown. After dinner, with the April evening a perfect seventy degrees, we walked south past the C&O Canal and underneath the Whitehurst Freeway to Georgetown Waterfront Park, then strolled along the eastern edge of the river, past the Watergate complex and the Kennedy Center, eventually ending up at the Lincoln Memorial. We walked around the Memorial to the side facing the Reflecting Pool and sat on the steps beneath the statue of Lincoln, looking toward the Washington Monument.

"You know, I can't remember a more perfect day and evening than this," I remarked. And it was true.

She smiled, reached over and held my hand. "Yes, it is nice," she said. "I want to remember this."

Before we parted company, we inscribed each other's numbers into our smartphones.

Naturally, I had misgivings. Why wasn't such an intelligent, attractive, immensely gifted young woman already spoken for? What did she see in me? Granted, I wasn't bad looking, I knew which fork to use in trendy French restaurants, and I could hold my own in most non-technical conversations—but compared to her, I was definitely lower-tier. I taught art... she *made* art!

I called her the next morning.

She had a recital the following week and was scheduled to

practice that morning at the Kennedy Center on their Steinway grand in the Concert Hall. She asked if I wanted to come by to listen.

What do you think I answered?

She had left my name at the front office, and I arrived there a half hour early. This being a practice session, the hall was, of course, completely empty. I chose the nearest seat to the piano in the front row, decided that was too close, and moved toward the back of the theater. In the vastness of the barren auditorium, sitting so far away didn't seem right, either. I finally settled on an aisle seat several rows from the front.

The grand piano was positioned at the center of the stage, and although it was an imposing instrument, it seemed dwarfed by the sheer size of a rostrum designed to accommodate an entire symphony. I couldn't imagine walking onto the stage to play in front of a full house: two thousand pairs of eyes intently watching your every movement, two thousand pairs of ears listening to every nuance of your performance.

She came out from the wings, accompanied by the concert hall's music director and stage manager. When she reached center stage, Iliana saw me and waved, walking over to the edge of the dais. "Hey! Thanks for coming. Were you able to find a good seat?"

"This fat guy next to me is crowding me a bit, but fortunately it's an aisle seat," I answered, suddenly worried that she might have overweight relatives.

Iliana laughed. "If he's hogging your armrest, let me know and I'll find you a better spot." She walked back to the two men and they talked a bit, then she sat down at the piano.

She played a collection of short pieces by Erik Satie, including three of his earlier works, the *Gymnopédies*. As Iliana played each composition, I recognized portions—although if asked then, I couldn't have identified the composer, much less provided any of the titles.

And although I had heard some of the pieces before, I had never heard them like this. The mastery of her touch, the lyricism of each note and chord reached into the deepest recesses of my soul. In her care, the Steinway seemed to become an extension of her own body: not an instrument to be played upon, but rather to become part of. As I listened, the cavernous space of the concert hall vanished and I was enveloped in a cocoon of pure introspection. I had experienced this same profound sensation while gazing at painted and sculpted masterpieces in galleries—it was why I had become an art historian—but never before with music.

I was spellbound, and I was quickly, inexorably, falling for her. I went to every practice I could. I attended every performance she gave. We quickly became close friends, then an item, and then a couple. At first, I thought my attraction was simply infatuation that would temper with time.

But it never did.

I was in heaven. Iliana was without question the best thing that had ever happened to me. She enhanced every aspect of my life. Obviously, my understanding and appreciation for music deepened, but it went far beyond that: my attitude was elevated; my vitality was invigorated; my universe was expanded; my world was brightened.

We spent whatever time we could together. Often, after her practice or performance, we would leave the Kennedy Center together and stroll over to the Lincoln Memorial, sitting on the steps overlooking the Reflecting Pool. I came to think of it as our spot.

She moved in with me in July, after we had been together about three months. With the money she saved in rent, she set about redecorating my spacious condominium loft near Logan Circle. The heavy shades that had come with the place were the first to go, replaced by sheer, translucent curtains and valances. She graced the hardwood flooring with large, brightly colored ornate afghan rugs that fit each room so perfectly, they seemed to have been custom-made.

Literally overnight, my bachelor pad was transformed, from a drab and characterless place-to-crash, into a bright and stimulating habitat. Light suddenly permeated every nook. What had been dark and confining was now light and airy, sensuously tactile, spiritually inspiring. For the first time, I actually enjoyed spending afternoons in the oversized two-story great room, feeling the natural radiant warmth permeating the entire area, listening to Iliana play her splendid Bechstein parlor grand, which dominated the room.

The greatest challenge was, of course, getting the Bechstein into the great room. As it was a loft, it was the top floor of the condo, and the freight elevator wasn't quite large enough to accommodate the grand piano. Even if it had been, the Bechstein wouldn't have fit through the front door. So, the only way to manage it was over the balcony in the front of the building. I had seen movies and commercials in which grand pianos are hoisted from the street to an upper-floor dwelling, but never witnessed it in person. I remembered thinking as I watched the movers struggle with the half-ton prized possession: I hope we never have to leave this place.

It never occurred to me that she might leave on her own. But leave she did, after three and a half years. She took some of her toiletries, most of her clothing, and all of her music.

She left the piano. I don't think that she intended it as a parting gift. It just wasn't possible to quietly leave in the middle of the night while a team of piano movers lowered the Bechstein over the balcony to the street, five floors below.

She became part of the exodus. The mad rush to... where? Anywhere but here.

It had happened a little before sunrise, our time. On the other side of the globe where it was already light, the sun had begun to slowly fade over the course of an hour, until it completely disappeared. At first, many had assumed it was a total eclipse... but the light never returned. In pre-dawn Washington, early risers expected it to begin turning brighter—which, of course, it didn't. The sun simply never showed up for its appointed rounds.

Actually, it did show up, but unless you knew exactly where to look, you wouldn't have seen it. A black disc against a black sky—imperceptible, save for the stars it eclipsed, gradually breaking the horizon and rising along its circumscribed path. Once the sustainer of life: now a massive, burned-out cinder.

Everything was completely dark. The electricity still worked, but the sky was black as pitch. It quickly turned unseasonably cool for late August—more like a mid-November day, or the crispness of an early spring night. The Earth, it turns out, retains a considerable amount of heat. I imagine that this is attributable to our atmosphere. Or, it might have something to do with our planet's magnetic field, which I understand is exceptionally strong. Or, it might be due to the oceans of red-hot magma boiling just beneath the crust. Whatever the reason, we didn't turn into a hunk of frozen detritus right away.

I put on some slippers and my robe, walked into the great room and clicked on the television, not knowing what to expect. Would anyone still be broadcasting?

It turned out that they were... some channels, anyway. All of the major networks were still on, and of course it was nonstop news. I imagine that, if I had a career as a journalist, this would have been the story to end all stories, in more ways than one. But what was there to report?

"This just in from our Washington bureau: the sun is still out."

click

"We have a correspondent in Boston right now—John, what's it like there?"

"Um, Katie, it's dark."

click

"Our intrepid meteorologist in Atlanta, Ken Banks, has this report. What can we expect, Ken?"

"Brian, we anticipate that it will continue to get colder. The good news is that you can see the entire Milky Way at eight-thirty a.m.!"

I'm joking, of course—it was a lot more serious than that, and much more disheartening. The reports were a hodgepodge of confusion and conjecture. Much of it centered on survival and the need to maintain order, for as long as possible. The president gave a special address from an undisclosed location, urging calm and assuring the public that the federal government was doing everything it could to assess the situation and formulate a plan of action.

The only question that mattered—the burning question, so to speak—was whether or not the sunlight might return. Had it simply snuffed out like a lit match, or was it more like the smoldering embers in a fireplace that might suddenly re-ignite with a burst of flame?

Most of the scientists interviewed said simply that they didn't know. One fellow, who looked like the archetypical mad scientist, with stooped shoulders draped in a white lab coat and wildly unkempt hair, postulated that this was a "cyclical event," as he termed it. He seemed confident in his calculations that the sun would eventually rekindle—in a few thousand years or so. Other scientists weren't so optimistic, if you could call it that. As in: not going to happen.

I turned off the TV.

From my studio condo I could see the traffic streaming out of Washington, all of it heading south. I suppose the theory was that the south would be warmer—after all, it's the south. But it's only warmer by virtue of being more in line with the sun… and the sun had gone out.

Probably the wisest course would have been to travel to some geothermal hotspot, like Iceland or Yellowstone, if you could get there. Or just remain hunkered down at home, and hope against hope that the heat stayed on indefinitely.

There was a lot of commotion: people throughout the condominium building were rushing about, yelling at each other, desperate to do something in response to this calamity.

Do what?

As for me, I was completely calm. After all, my world had just come to an end. I went to the kitchen, poured myself a glass of cognac from the bottle I had been saving for special occasions, walked back into the great room and stood at the balcony window for a while, watching the red river of taillights on the cars heading southward. I turned back into the room and sat down in my favorite chair—a wingback we owned…

actually, Iliana owned... studying the Bechstein, remembering the enchanted sounds she had charmed from it with her impossibly delicate fingers. Now the piano was forever silent. A darkly stained, impotent hulk.

I sat there for some time, my depression deepening. What was the use? We were all going to die, apparently sooner rather than later. All that was taught would be lost, all that was created would be destroyed. Perhaps the scientists were right: that the creation of the universe was cyclical, and all of this would happen once again billions of years from now, and again after that. But to what end?

I slowly stood and walked back to the balcony, opening the doors, the cooler air immediately apparent. Was it better to die a slow, freezing death, or to end it quickly, here and now? I went to the edge of the tiled concrete and gazed down at the sidewalk, five stories below. A leap from the railing and it was over. Finis. Or maybe not—what if fifty feet wasn't enough? Then enduring agony...

I looked almost due south at the Washington Monument, still brightly illuminated. That massive obelisk certainly was tall enough. I had taken the elevator to the top a few times when I first moved to DC, playing tourist on the Mall. There wasn't any observation deck, and the windows were impossible to climb through. Was that intentional, to prevent suicide jumps?

I folded my arms against the chill. Who was I kidding? Fifty feet or five hundred, I'd never jump.

I went back inside. For an instant, I thought about calling the school to tell them that I wouldn't be in today. Then I caught myself and laughed out loud.

Crap.

I finished my cognac, put on the one pair of thermals I owned under winter-weight clothes and left the condo.

I walked the ten blocks to the Mall, passing by the White House. Other than the lines of cars crawling out of the city, the streets were eerily empty. There was a placard lying on the ground near the wrought iron fence—the sort carried by the perpetual protestors and assorted crazies who encamp across the street from the presidential mansion.

It read: "Repent! The End is Near—Matthew 24:14".

Now that it was actually coming true, there was no one holding the sign, declaring, "I told you so!" Evidently, when the going got extreme, the extreme got going somewhere else, most probably down south.

Was the placard right? Was this punishment for our sins? Natural disasters occurred all the time. Some people attributed them to God-ordained punishment, though without any evidence that the victims were more sinful or less deserving of a peaceful life than anyone else.

If natural disasters *were* retribution, then it was safe to say that this one was the mother of all paybacks. What had we done wrong? In Genesis, God punished mankind for our sins, yet prepared us for a new beginning through Noah and his ark. But where was the ark this time? Beneath the ground? I wondered whether there were vast networks of underground tunnels constructed to sustain people—and plants and animals—vestiges of the Cold War in preparation for a nuclear winter. How long could a nuclear winter last? Ten years? Twenty? Even if it lasted a century, it was still finite. It certainly wasn't on par with the sun going out.

What would be the purpose of divine retribution if no one survived to learn the lesson?

Perhaps our time had simply run out. It reminded me of a poster I had in my dorm room at college. It featured a cartoon-like scribble of a guy with a crown, saying: "Earth, this is God! I want you out by the end of the month—I have a client who's interested in the property." I wondered whether the new owner was aware that it no longer came with a sunny view.

When I reached the Mall, I turned east and proceeded to the National Gallery of Art. I figured that the entrance would be locked, but to my surprise the door was open. One guard stood near the entrance, an elderly black man.

"May I help you?" he asked.

"The sun's gone out," I said.

"I know," he nodded. "A cryin' shame."

"I wanted to visit the gallery one last time," I said, by way of explanation.

He waved me in. "You have yourself a nice visit."

I wandered through the halls, gazing at the art as if for the last time, which of course it was. I had my favorites—Rodin's *The Thinker*, Degas' *Little Dancer*, Eakin's *Biglin Brothers Racing*, Homer's *Breezing Up*, Bellows' *Both Members of This Club*, Henri's *Girl Seated by the Sea*, and many more, and I made certain that I saw each one. I had the place to myself. Apparently no one else in Washington wanted to spend a portion of their suddenly abbreviated time on Earth looking at old sculptures and paintings. All alone, with only my thoughts to keep me company, I could think of no better way to await eternity. Actually, I could think of a much better way, but she was gone.

Wandering from one wing to another, I eventually arrived at the French Impressionists. As I entered the room with the Monet, I stopped short: although the gallery was fully illuminated by electric lights discretely placed around its circumference, gone were the shafts of sunbeams through the skylight that had enveloped Iliana the first time I saw her.

I sat on the bench in the center of the large room and pondered Monet's masterpiece. As I mentioned earlier, he had painted it not long after his young wife, Camille, had passed away. Monet animated the painting with the stylized pointillist dashes of the Impressionist movement, depicting the brilliant yellows of blossoming sunflowers amid cascades of various plants in bloom—the vibrant array filling the canvas to either side of a shaded pathway, its steps leading up to the house in the background. But even with the captivating splashes of colorful flora that filled the canvas, my eye was repeatedly drawn to the central figure of a small child dressed all in white, standing at the base of the steps next to his little wagon.

Three tiny speckles of reddish umber defined the child's eyes and mouth. The National Gallery's brochure explained that, in this painting, Monet was more interested in decoration than description. How I begged to differ! My heart ached for this diminutive, solitary figure, his posture slightly tilted with a child's innocence, facing the viewer (and Monet). Perhaps my interpretation was prejudiced, knowing as I did that this was the artist's youngest son, Michel, recently turned two. My eyes welled with tears thinking about Monet's now-motherless child… about finality and lost opportunity and love no longer shared.

And then I realized that I was projecting onto this child. I wiped my eyes, feeling foolish. What time was it? I checked my cell phone: 11:16 am. It seemed much later. I stared at the phone for several minutes and then called her number.

No answer. After several rings I was carted to voicemail. I

started blurting into the phone:

"Ili, I hope you get this message. I woke up and you were… I didn't realize that you… I don't know. I just wish we could have… talked about it before you left. You wouldn't believe where I am right now! Believe it or not, I'm in the National Gallery, sitting here in the Monet Room, looking right at his painting of the garden with those sunflowers, the one with all those colors. That's a great description I know… *all* of his stuff is filled with colors. His 'stuff'! Do you remember saying that? That was so perfect, when you said that. It made me…"

I paused for a moment.

"Hey, nobody else is here… I mean, duh! I'm surprised this place is even open. I don't know why I came down here… I guess I couldn't think of anything else to do. I couldn't sit around the condo… it was, I don't know… it felt empty, being there all by myself."

I paused again, trying to figure out what I wanted to say.

"You know, I think that maybe we could have talked about this. Maybe if we'd, you know, discussed it a bit…"

The message service cut me off.

The lights suddenly flickered. It occurred to me that, if the electricity went out, I would be stuck in the center of the National Gallery of Art in absolute darkness. I assumed that the museum must have a backup generator or, at the very least, some battery-powered emergency lights in the event of a blackout. A blackout! I gave a scornful laugh. Even if there were emergency lights, at some point those would fail, too.

As if in response, the lights flickered again.

After the power inevitably failed—what then? The world would continue its steady decline toward absolute zero. Even if underground survival chambers did exist, they'd be filled and sealed soon enough. On the surface, there would be an increasingly desperate need for heat and light: fire. Everything that could burn would become fuel. Eventually, the Kennedy Center's concert grand, and the marvelous Bechstein sitting five floors above Logan Circle, would be consumed. Ultimately, even these paintings would be tossed into the flames.

These were not pleasant thoughts, even if I hadn't been an art history professor. In the end, it didn't matter, did it? What would be the purpose of keeping masterpieces intact if no one was left to appreciate them? To leave them behind for some alien archeologists to uncover, so that they might appreciate what had come before: the legacy of humankind's vision and quest? Besides, long before any visitors might possibly arrive, it would get so cold that the paints and canvas would crack into a thousand pieces and turn to dust. What was the use? The sun went out. End of story.

I sat a bit longer in the complete silence, then stood and slowly walked through the galleries back to the entrance. The guard was still there.

"Did you have a nice tour?" he asked.

"Yes, yes, I did. Will you be open tomorrow?"

He shrugged. "I haven't heard otherwise, so I expect so."

I started to leave, then turned back. "You know that the sun went out."

He nodded. "So I've heard."

"You should be home with your family, not here."

The guard let out a sigh, took off his cap and scratched his bald head. "No family to speak of. Besides, I'd just get in the way."

"No children or grandchildren?"

He shook his head. "Wife passed away a few years ago.

Kids all grew up and moved away long before that. All I got is my dog and my cat."

"No other relatives? No drinking buddies or lady friends?"

He shook his head again. "Don't you worry about me. You're young. You must have friends and family. What are *you* doing here? I'm here because it's my job. What's your excuse?"

"I'm an art history professor—I teach French Impression- ism." Then I realized that, considering the circumstances, it wasn't much of a reason. I looked down at the polished stone floor. "My... girlfriend left me this morning."

The guard clicked his tongue. "My, my, that's a cryin' shame. And today of all days!"

"Well, she left before the sun came up, so I don't think she knew."

"Still, that's awful bad timing. Any idea where she went?"

I shook my head.

"Have you tried calling her?" he asked. "Maybe she didn't go far. She got family around here?"

"No family that I know of. She's from Northern Europe. I tried reaching her a little while ago, but she didn't answer. I left a message."

He studied my face. "You like her a lot, I can tell. You should try again. Couldn't hurt."

"I don't know why she left. We were together for three and a half years and things seemed fine."

"Appears not. If I were you, I'd head home and keep trying her number. Seems to me you two should be together now."

I waved goodbye. "Thanks. Maybe I'll see you tomorrow."

He put his cap back on and gave me a little salute. "I expect I'll be here, if we all don't freeze solid before then."

I walked westward back along the Mall and then turned

north up 14th Street. It was just after noon, and black as night. Cars were still streaming out of the District, traveling southward and westward toward the bridges across the Potomac into Virginia. It was slow going, of course, and much more orderly than I would have expected. People were still in too much shock, I surmised, to waste time honking horns or succumbing to bouts of road rage. Or maybe they were just resigned to their fate—like the survivors of an earthquake, tsunami, tornado, or any other sudden disaster.

It was definitely colder. More like late November, now. I still didn't need the thermals I was wearing—but who knew? It wasn't like this had happened before. I wondered whether it was actually any warmer closer to the equator. It must be a bit more temperate, I surmised, if only because it was warmer to begin with. But by how much and for how long?

All of the stores along 14th street were closed, of course. There was a food truck parked on K Street named *Anita's Real Empanadas* that appeared to be open.

I walked up to the window. In addition to empanadas, they served assorted Latin American fast food dishes. The prices were reasonable.

"Why are you open?" I asked.

A young woman in a full-length apron leaned out the window, wiping the counter with a cloth. "Why not?"

"The sun's gone out," I pointed out.

"All the more reason to treat yourself to the best empanadas this side of the Mississippi. We're running a special—you get three, coffee's free."

"That sounded rehearsed."

"Gee, ya think?" she retorted. "Look, you gonna order? I'm kinda busy here."

I glanced behind me. No one else was in line. "I'll have three chicken empanadas and a large coffee."

"Comin' right up," she said, and turned away to prepare the food. She was the only person in the truck.

A minute later, she handed me the bag with the empanadas and the cup of coffee. In the slightly chilled air, steam was escaping from both. "That'll be nine seventy-five."

I reached into my pocket and pulled out a ten, handing it to her. "Keep the change."

"Oh, a big tipper!" she exclaimed. "Wow, thanks, Mr. Trump! Come back anytime!"

Was she in denial, I wondered, or was she just trying to stay positive—and sane? Or had she already flipped out? As I continued up 14th Street, I opened the bag and sniffed. They seemed fine... in fact the aroma was wonderful. Maybe I should eat myself to death... order everything I had always avoided, to make up for lost opportunities. What did it matter now? What did anything matter, now that Iliana was gone?

I reached the condo and took the elevator up to my floor. No one remained in the halls running about, screaming and wailing. I thought I could hear some muffled sobs behind closed doors, but it could just as well have been crazed chuck-ling. Everyone would face the reality differently, I supposed.

Entering my suite, I held my breath.

She wasn't there.

I slowly exhaled, devastated but not surprised. On the bright side, now I had three empanadas all to myself. If only there had been a bright side.

I ate the meal in silence, forcing myself to finish the last pastry, even though I was full. Both the empanadas and the coffee were excellent. It occurred to me that this was the first dinner I had eaten alone in more than three years. We had always coordinated our schedules to be home together at dinnertime. What was I saying—dinnertime? It was a little after noon! It just felt like dinner in the dark.

Home together at dinnertime. When Iliana was there—breakfast, lunchtime, dinnertime, whenever—it was home. Bright and warm and comforting. Now, it was just a place to die.

As I sipped my coffee, I studied the Bechstein and pictured it sitting alone upon a barren Earth, every other vestige of mankind having long since faded away into the rock. The planet was spinning in the void: lifeless, dark and cold. Inevitably the piano, too, would crumble into dust. But, at a moment in time in the universe, it had delivered affirmation to the wonder of life, in the hands of one who understood its worth.

I finished the coffee and wandered aimlessly around the loft. For some reason, I ended up in the walk-in closet in our bedroom. Iliana had taken most of her clothing, but there were a few items left on their padded hangers. There was the black evening gown she had worn last year for a Ravel concert. It had a slight tear in one seam, which I guessed was why she hadn't packed it. There were a few sweaters—she could have used those now—as well as a handful of blouses and dresses. I gathered them together in my hands and pressed my face into them, wanting to smell her, to feel her near me.

I walked back into the bedroom, sat on the edge of the queen-sized bed, pulled my phone out of my pocket and called her number. No answer. When the voicemail kicked in, I started talking immediately:

"Ili, please come back. I can't deal with this alone. I need you here… please come back."

I hung up.

Where did she go? Did she know something like this would happen? Some sort of premonition? How on earth could someone have a premonition about this?

I glanced at the clock on the bed stand: 1:02. I laughed scornfully. What did it matter anymore? The brand was eClock—soon to be noClock when the electricity failed. What did it matter? Even a sundial was useless now! What good was time anymore? Man used to gauge his life by the sun: the days began and ended with the passage of the sun above or below the horizon. Clocks may have dispensed with that reverence, but we still gauged a day by the cycle of light. Dawn: time to rise. Noon: time to lunch. Dusk: time to dine. Night: time to retire.

Now there was only the night. Bye-bye circadian rhythms. Bye-bye routines and rituals. Bye-bye everything. No Armageddon before the eschaton... no nuclear apocalypse or invading armies from Hell. Just lights out.

I sat there for a while, my thoughts a jumbled mass of despair. I glanced at the clock again: 1:10.

1:10 pm in the middle of the night.

I made myself another cup of coffee, for the first time in my life seriously mindful about wasting energy to heat the pot. I brought the cup into the dimly-lit great room, sat in the wingback chair and sipped the warm brew, studying the Bechstein, recalling the amazing music it had produced—she had produced. Without her, it was... what? An elaborate, impractical piece of furniture. I walked over to the bench and sat down, lifted the cover and lightly caressed the keys, then gingerly tapped Middle C. The resonant note was clean, pure... and bland. I tapped it several times, filling the room with the monotonous tone. A nice enough sound, but by itself character-less. I suddenly felt as though I was violating the sanctity of the instrument, and carefully shut the cover.

I finished my coffee and sat there… staring, thinking, re-gretting.

I walked out the double-doors onto the balcony. Cars were still streaming out of the city, though not as many. My guess was that people were realizing it didn't matter where they were—Washington, Florida, or Ecuador for that matter—and they began to question if they really wanted to spend the last moments of their lives stuck in a thousand-mile-long traffic jam on I-95.

I wondered if Iliana was crawling along the interstate in the Lexus.

I wondered whether she was still driving anywhere.

I wondered where she might be.

I wondered if she was thinking about me.

I wondered about that time I first saw her.

I wondered whether the National Gallery was still open.

I put on my winter coat and left the condo, walking back down 14th Street. I still didn't need the heavy garment, but it made me feel better.

As I passed K Street, I noticed that the empanada food truck was gone, and wondered whether the young woman was home with her family. I figured that she must have a family to be with—her parents, a boyfriend, maybe a husband and kids. My own parents had passed away fairly young, both of them to cancer. I didn't have any siblings. Maybe that was a blessing now… not having to worry about anyone.

Anyone other than Iliana. I wondered again where she might be, and if she was with her family. Had she flown back to Estonia? Were the planes flying? I realized that I hadn't noticed any traffic out of National Airport. Usually the jets could be seen either taking off or landing along the Potomac. I assumed they must be grounded: possible navigation issues without the sun; or perhaps the pilots and air traffic controllers simply hadn't come to work. Wherever she was, I hoped she was alright.

When I arrived at the National Gallery, the entrance was still open. The guard was inside, standing near the narrow tables where they inspected bags.

"Well, hello again," he smiled at me. "Back for another look?"

I shrugged. "I suppose. I don't know. I just needed to get out of my place."

He folded his arms, his brow now furrowed. "She still didn't call?"

I shook my head. "I tried reaching her again, but no answer. I left another message."

As before, he took off his cap and scratched his head. Then he motioned for me to follow him over to a large oak desk by the wall. I sat down on a nearby bench as he settled into the desk's wooden swivel chair.

"Now that's a puzzle, she not calling back. You two have a fight yesterday?"

I thought about the day before and shook my head. "Not that I can remember. She came home around five and started making dinner. I was already home, grading papers. We had dinner, then we watched the news, and then I graded some more papers while she played a piece by Ravel—*Scarbo*, I think it's called—from his *Gaspard de la Nuit*."

"Ravel, huh? He's a composer, right?"

I laughed. "You could say that. French composer, lived about a century ago."

"So what does she play? Piano?"

I nodded.

"She play good?"

"Didn't I mention it before? She's the featured piano soloist with the National Symphony."

He let out a low whistle. "Lordy! No, you didn't mention that. No wonder you're fond of her! So you sat there and you listened while she played, that right?"

I nodded again.

"That happens a lot, I take it? I mean, you sitting there and listening while she plays?"

I nodded once more.

"So, what happens when she finishes—you clap or something?"

I laughed again. "Well, I used to. But that seemed kind of patronizing, so not anymore. Now I just sit and listen."

He studied me for a moment. "How do you mean, you sit there and listen? Do you watch her play, like you're the audience?"

I thought back to that first practice I went to at the Kennedy Center, and the many performances I had attended since. "I guess I did, early on, but I haven't done that for a long time. Now I just sit and read the newspaper or a magazine, or use my laptop, or work on school materials—like the papers I mentioned."

He leaned forward, resting his arms on the desktop. "So, you got this amazingly talented young lady—this *virtuoso*—living with you and cooking you meals, and I bet she probably decorated your whole place and whatnot, and you're just eating her food and grading papers while she serenades you, that about right?"

I shrugged. "Well, when you put it that way…"

He leaned back in his chair. "How would *you* put it?"

"I don't know," I protested. "It's her job—the piano playing, I mean. She wasn't serenading me."

The guard leaned forward again. "Son, she was serenading your sorry ass."

I thought about that, about how her music made me feel. "You're telling me that I was ignoring her?"

He leaned back once more. "You tell *me*, professor," he said. "Did you?"

I sat there across the desk from this bald-headed National Gallery security guard and thought about it.

I thought about it a long time.

"I guess I took a lot for granted," I admitted.

He folded his hands in his lap. "So, how you gonna fix this?"

I looked down at the gallery's marble floor. "I think it's too late for that. She's not even returning my calls."

He was quiet for a moment, and then he said: "R-E-S-P-E-C-T"

I looked up at him. "You mean that song? The Aretha Franklin one? What about it?"

"Actually, Otis Redding wrote it, but yeah—Aretha made it hers. It was on her album *I Never Loved a Man the Way I Loved You.*"

As I'm sure he could tell from my blank expression, I was completely lost.

He shook his head and sighed. "You teach art, so you give lectures about artists and their art, that right?"

"Yes, of course."

"So you like to study art, and you like to discuss art."

I nodded.

The guard put his cap back on and stood up. "Take a walk with me," he said.

He led and I followed, down the East Sculpture Hall with its neo-classical statuary and into the series of galleries devoted to Nineteenth Century French artists. But instead of entering the gallery with Monet's garden painting, we turned to the right into a gallery devoted to works by the American Impressionist, Mary Cassatt.

"As I recall, you said you taught French Impressionism," the guard said. "Well, Miss Cassatt here studied in France, isn't that so?"

"Yes," I nodded, "she studied under Pissarro and Degas, and she was a contemporary of Renoir, Monet, Cezanne—most of the great French Impressionists. That was possible because her parents were quite wealthy, and they could afford to send her abroad for much of her early education. While studying in Paris, she attended an exhibition featuring works by several renowned artists, including Delacroix, Courbet, and… "

"That's fine," the guard cut me off. "I'm sure you know a damn sight more about the life of this lady than I do. But I want to talk with you about this painting, the one with the people in the boat."

He pointed to the wall facing us, featuring a painting measuring about four feet wide and three feet high. It was *The Boating Party*—one of the works I had made a point of visiting earlier. It portrayed a couple with their child in a small skiff out on a river or lake: the man, dressed in dark blue, faced away from the viewer as he handled the oars; the woman, wearing the long dress of the period and sporting a lovely spring hat, was holding their young child on her lap. Unlike the diminutive, solitary child standing at the center of Monet's sunflower garden, this child was held in her mother's lap and seemed very contented.

"*The Boating Party*, of course," I said, walking over to the ornately-framed work and automatically launching into the lecture I had delivered dozens of times to my students. "Painted by Cassatt around eighteen ninety-four. Oil on canvas. It's a young family on an outing in a boat, notably bold in its composition—notice how the lines of force created by the man's left arm and the oar direct our attention to the child, who is positioned at the center of the composition. This is reinforced by the arrow created in the outlines of the sail, which redirect us to the child. There are strong Impressionist elements in the treatment of the water, with marked Japanese influences in the patterning of the woman's dress among other things, such as..."

"Yes, very good, professor," the guard said, cutting me off again. "I'd take notes, but I forgot my pen. I wanted to ask you about the people in the picture."

"What do you want to know?"

"You said they're a family. What makes you so sure of that? Couldn't this fellow just be rowing them somewhere, like those gondoliers do in Venice?"

"Not likely. Dressed the way she is and with the child, she wouldn't have hired some fellow with a skiff to row them across the water. It's pretty evident that this is an outing and they're having a leisurely ride in a boat."

He nodded. "Okay, so it's two folks and their kid. I got that. Why did Miss Cassatt paint this?"

I shrugged. "Why does anyone paint anything? I'm guessing that she must have been inspired by something. Maybe she'd gone on a boat outing, and wanted to capture the feeling. Maybe these were friends of hers, and she had this mental image of them on the boat, and decided that it made a nice subject. Maybe it just allowed her to play around with some of those compositional elements I mentioned…"

"I think maybe it has more to it than that," he said. "Let's talk about the people. Which one do we look at?"

I studied the work. "Well, all three," I said. "But as I mentioned, the composition directs our attention to the young child. Even the curved lines of the skiff point to her. She's the most colorful element in the entire painting and, as I also mentioned, she's the centerpiece."

"Where is the child looking?"

"At the man," I answered.

"And where is the lady looking?"

"Also at the man."

The guard paused, studying me, not the painting. "And where is the man looking?"

I examined the work again. "At the child," I volunteered, "which makes sense, compositionally."

"You told me that everything points to the child. If that's so, then why isn't the woman looking down at her child? Why is she looking straight at the man?"

I was becoming uncomfortable with his questions. How was I supposed to know why Cassatt chose to paint it that way? "Look, I don't know—maybe it helped tie them together." I thought about that a bit more. "If she also looked at the child, then the painting becomes more of an adoration—almost like a nativity scene, I would imagine."

The guard thought about this, then shrugged. "Okay. I think that's a stretch, but let's say it's true. So, why didn't she paint it that way? Miss Cassatt made a whole mess of paintings showing mothers with their children. That sort of became her trademark, if I'm not mistaken. And in every one of them, the mother is looking at her child—like that nativity scene you just talked about. The brochure we hand out says she was very fond of the *Madonna and Child* motif."

He smiled. "I like that word—*motif*. Real artsy-sounding. What I'm saying is, I want to know why she's looking at the man instead in this painting."

It was my turn to shrug. "I guess we'll never know."

"Maybe not," he conceded. "How would you describe her expression?"

I walked up to the painting and peered closely.

"Not so close, sir," He strode over to me with his arm extended. "You need to take a step back, sir."

I dutifully backed away. The guard slapped his knees and let out a laugh.

"Sorry, force of habit," he said. "You go ahead and get as close as you want, professor. I trust you."

I peered at the work once more. "I'd say that the woman is looking at him with affection, but also a hint of apprehension," I offered.

The guard nodded. "The experts say that there's a lot of tension in this painting. So you agree that she's focused on him?"

I nodded.

"But he isn't focused on her?"

"No," I said. "He's focused on the child."

"His child?"

"Possibly. No way of knowing. It's definitely her child."

"Definitely her child," he repeated. "So, it's like the child is a part of her?"

I looked again at the progeny splayed in her lap and nodded. "Sure, in a way, the child is certainly part of her."

He gestured toward the painting. "You know, Miss Cassatt here was very talented. I know that you know a lot about her, but I've listened to the docents and the guides over the years, and I've done a little reading up on her myself. She spent her whole life trying to prove herself in a man's world. She never got married and she never had any kids—even so, like I said, she spent most of her time painting portraits of mothers with their children. It's almost like she was fixating on these ladies and their daughters."

He paused for a moment pondering the work.

"I've spent a lot of time looking at this painting. When you're on duty here and you're posted in a room, you spend a lot of time studying the art. Now, I'm no professor of anything—no formal training in art, never even gone into a gallery except for this one. Maybe I've looked at this painting a bit too long and maybe I'm seeing things that aren't really there, but it strikes me that this is like a self-portrait. I think that's Miss Cassatt herself sitting in that boat, and this child she's holding is supposed to be her work. Hell, she was forty-nine when she painted this. She knew she'd never have any children of her own... her paintings were her children. She's displaying her child proudly—it's all brightly lit. But Miss Cassatt painted herself in shadow."

He gestured toward the painting again. "She looks to me like she's hoping the man will look up at her, to see *her*."

He looked back at me. "Maybe there comes a point where

you got to look up, too."

He peered at his watch. "And I got to get back to my station. But you go ahead and study the painting some more. I'll see you back up front when you're done." He turned and walked out of the gallery, leaving me standing alone with the Cassatt.

Being an art history professor, I couldn't just walk away. Why indeed was the woman gazing at the man, while the man was looking at the child? Was this more than just a boating outing?

The child was without question the brightest object in the painting, drenched in sunlight. On the other hand, the woman was cast in shadow, far outshone by the child. She was an attractive woman—even beautiful. She seemed thoughtful, understanding, and wonderfully human. But she was subordinate to the offspring in her lap.

All of the directional lines in the work pointed to the child, none to the woman herself. Even the man, whom she gazed at endearingly, hopefully, didn't see her. All of his attention—indeed, all of his actions—were directed at the child.

I sat down on the bench in the middle of the room and thought about what I wanted to say. I pulled out my cell phone and dialed her number. It rang several times and once again carted me to voicemail.

"Ili," I said. "There's something I need to tell you that I've never told you. I love your music. I love how it makes me feel, I love the way it lifts me up and carries me along on its beautiful sound, how it transports me to another world, how it paints dazzling canvases and reaches deep into my soul. But even if you had never played a single note, what I truly love about you... is you. My world is empty without you in it—cold and dark and meaningless. You mean everything to me, Iliana. I love *you*."

I hung up, and then slowly walked back through the museum to the entrance. The guard was seated at his desk.

"You didn't linger long," he said.

"I didn't have to. I think I figured it out."

"Oh, is that right? And what would that be?"

"I called Iliana again and left another message."

He winked at me. "Good for you. See you tomorrow?"

I nodded. "If we don't freeze solid before then. Thanks."

He gave me his little salute. "You take care, now."

I reentered the darkness. Instead of turning right toward 14th Street, I walked out to the middle of the Mall, the Capitol to my left and the Washington Monument to my right. Both were still brightly lit. I decided that their lights must not be on timers, since it was somewhere between two and three pm. Perhaps daylight sensors controlled the lights, or perhaps they were manually operated. It seemed like a waste of electricity, which now was a very precious commodity. Wouldn't it be best to conserve whatever energy we could?

Then again... lit up, they served as beacons of hope, however futile. But hope was waning. Standing alone in the middle of the Mall at the center of the nation's capital, in the total blackness of that day, I felt a curtain of finality descend upon me. Like everyone else, I was going to die soon. Yet I felt an odd sense of relief, as if I had settled accounts. I didn't want to die—there were, of course, countless things I still wanted to do—but I couldn't shake this feeling of closure.

She wasn't coming back. I had finally said what needed to be said, what I should have said a long time ago. A farewell from the heart... what more could one desire?

I walked toward the monument, wending my way between the cars still heading southward on 14th Street, and then I continued around it down to the World War II Memorial, also brightly lit. I sat on the concrete, looking at the pillars and wreaths for each state, with the majestic 50-story obelisk towering behind, atop its shallow hill.

A memorial to sacrifice. Hundreds of thousands killed. Lives cut short... but for a greater good, not in vain. Now billions would soon perish—to what end? What good was the sacrifice of anyone or anything, in the past or the present?

What was the lesson? Perhaps... perhaps there was no lesson.

Could that be the lesson?

I sat there for some time, mulling this thought, then headed west, past the Vietnam Memorial and the Reflecting Pool, until I stood at the bottom of the steps leading to the Lincoln Memorial, where Iliana and I had enjoyed so many beautiful evenings after her rehearsals and concerts.

I slowly climbed the steps. A lot of history had taken place here: Martin Luther King Jr's *I Have a Dream* speech was probably the most famous. A dream... that's all it was, our little life, as Shakespeare had written in *The Tempest*.

I sat in the middle of the upper portion of steps, looking back east at the monument and the mall, the still-illuminated dome of the Capitol in the distance. I was the only person there. I imagined that everyone else must have something better to do with their last moments than to sit on some cold steps beneath a giant statue of Abraham Lincoln.

In the stillness and solitude, after a very long while, I finally drifted off to sleep. I dreamt of Monet's two young children, and Cassatt's many paintings of mother and child. I dreamt of them embracing their children on their laps, combing their hair, holding their tiny hands.

I started to awaken.

Someone was holding my hand.

"Hey," she said.

I smiled, still half-asleep. "I missed you."

"I know," she answered. "I missed you, too."

I sat up and hugged her, and we watched as the dawn broke and the sun inexorably rose behind the Capitol dome.

And there was light.

About the Authors

Asher Roth

Mr. Roth is a professional writer and illustrator. His previous books include *The Selfish Shellfish*, a fully-illustrated picture book for toddlers through early-elementary, and the YA sci-fi novel, *Serendipity*, published under his pen name, B. G. Holmsted. He attended the University of Virginia as an Echols Scholar, where he served as graphics editor of the university's literary arts journal, *Rivanna*. Meet him on his Facebook page or LinkedIn.

David W. Brooks

Mr. Brooks is a newspaperman from New England.

Bungalow Stokes

Bungalow Stokes has published, under various names, political opinion pieces, sports articles, journal articles on subjects as varied as education and micro-miniature circuit board repair, and poetry (for *Amelia* and *DEROS*). His pen name harkens to that most melancholy of idealists, Elliot Isaac Stokes, and the hovel he lived in when he worked in the oil fields of Elk City, Oklahoma.

Made in the USA
Columbia, SC
08 July 2017